LEAF

by

William Sells

Illustrated by Michael Bracco

To Kaleb,
Enjoy the Adventure!

Will

Book editing by Elizabeth Humphrey

www.bookwormediting.com Littleton, Colorado USA

Book packaging and design by Jacqui Terry

Kitchener, Ontario CANADA

www.jacquiterry.com

Art work by Michael Bracco

Baltimore, Maryland USA

www.spaghettikiss.com

Library of Congress: 2012951065

Author Dedication

To my wonderful wife, Yovi, who is teaching me about love, commitment, hard work, courage, integrity, compassion, selflessness, and truth. Thankfully, I am still in training.

This story is also dedicated to my three lovely and loving daughters, Gillian, Lindsay, and Sophia, who show me that every morning is brand new, and that life is a wondrous adventure when seen through their eyes.

And to my mom who believed I would someday live up to my potential.

Special thanks are also due to Dr. Martin Gordon for his experienced guidance, fervent support, and frightening faith in sending an unedited manuscript to Mbedzi Publishing; to my StoryMash cohort, Jim (Nash) Becker, for his keen wit, sharp eye, and blunt honesty; to the extraordinarily creative artist Michael Bracco for bringing all of the characters to life (including his new baby girl, Amelia), and to Karen Anderson, Elizabeth Humphrey and Jacqui Terry at Mbedzi Publishing for giving Leaf a loving home.

Thank you all!

PRELUDE

The ant queen sighed and slowly slid her large frame from her throne in order to see for herself. It wasn't that she didn't believe the reports—she had plenty of proof the reports were true—but she only trusted her own eyes for this sort of thing.

Smoke had filled the caverns of her domain more than once in recent weeks, and the ground shook so badly entire chambers and passageways had collapsed. Something was disturbing her realm from up above—again.

She boarded the transport drones and was lifted high above the mounds. It didn't take long for her to see what was causing the disturbance. It wasn't the water this time, but it was nearly as disruptive. Ten seconds later she descended, disembarked, and headed back to her chambers. An aide scurried to join her as she dragged herself down the corridor.

"Your commands, My Lady?" her aide inquired.

"What do you think?" she scolded. "We are moving—we are leaving—we are packing up and heading away from this madness. Complete migration to Elkhorn! Now! Move!"

The aide turned to head topside.

"Wait! I'm not done with you! Summon General Little and tell him to point his good antennae toward the center of the forest and find those floaters. It's time for revenge. I want their land. I want their resources. I want their respect, and I want their young breaking their backs in service to me!"

The aide turned again to leave.

"And," the queen added, as she rubbed her voluminous tummy, "I want a cricket sandwich."

CHAPTER ONE

CATCHING AIR

"Leaf! Come on!"

Twig hung suspended in the air for a moment before he flipped to catch a breeze up to the next level of the tree. He yelled again.

"Leaf!"

"I'm coming as soon as Nut moves out of the way!" Leaf shouted up to Twig and then looked at his friend Nut, who stood in front of him on the branch shaking harder than a regular leaf in a cold March wind.

"I don't like flipping up," Nut whined. "I don't mind floating down, but I don't like flipping up. I get dizzy, lose my bearings and hit my head on branches." He touched the side of his half-an-acorn helmet.

"That's why we gave you the helmet," Leaf assured. "Look, going up is the same as going down, only it's backwards."

Nut wasn't convinced.

"Let's go, Nut, before we're late for school!" Twig said.

Nut didn't budge. He looked up at Twig, felt for wind speed, looked behind him at Leaf, looked down, and then back up to Twig. He wanted to tell Leaf to go ahead, when Leaf suddenly grabbed him and leapt from the branch. Nut screamed, but before he could thoroughly panic, Leaf flipped them both, caught the rising air and landed safely next to Twig.

"D...d...don't do that again," Nut stammered, but Leaf wasn't there. He was already racing Twig through the branches to see who would be the first to school.

Nut watched them go and wished he was as fast and agile as his friends. Leaf was tall for his age and the strongest of the three. Twig was wiry but quite an able athlete. They flipped and floated effortlessly through the trees, and as living leaves go, they seemed to be cut from the same branch as the great Leaves of Old—the defenders of the Tree—the heroes of the Forest. The Legend Scroll listed their names—each one a leader of his generation. First, there was The Old Guard:

Hardy Hardknot

Timber Thickbranch

Gnarlie Knocknee

Curly Longroot

Crooked Lowstem (who wasn't liked at all and didn't reign long)

Greenlie Bowhanger

Ashton Stormhold

Cord Stackmount

Burley Barkbeater

Anson the Antthumper

Bastion the Brownstick

These were the Leaves of Old who established the Colony and defended it and the Tree against all their enemies: leaf-munching caterpillars, marauding ants, and pulp-eating termites. They passed the torch to the next set of leaders, called The New Guard. These were the ones who led and defended the Colony but then directed the great explorations:

Grover the Gatherer

Hawthorn the Harvester

Piney the Green (who built the first little boats)

Tiny the Green (Piney's youngest son, who built the first long-boats for travel)

Oakley the Reacher (the great explorer who first charted the streams, brooks, and creeks of the forest)

Erin the Bold Leaf (who first sailed to the harbor of the Coastals—the people who build houses and ships)

And last but not least was the leaf Colony's current sire, Erin's son, Eric the Red Leaf. Eric was the first to sail past the Coastal's harbor and out to the sea. He charted the shoreline of the land that held the forest, and he was also Leaf's father.

Nut slowly ambled along a sturdy branch and practiced reciting the names using the melody of an old nursery rhyme. He needed to memorize the list for the school's Scroll Exam, but couldn't quite do it till Leaf suggested the rhyme.

"Hardy Hardknot we hardly knew…..Timber Thickbranch was number two….Gnarlie Knocknee bent to the floor…Curly Longroot was number…."

Nut froze. "The Scroll Exam! School! I'm going to be late!"

He took three hurried steps and tripped on the first tiny knot his toes encountered. He fell off the branch, but didn't worry. He liked floating and was rather good at it. He slowly drifted down through the first few levels nicely, and was fairly proud of himself, until a cross-breeze caught him and sent him sideways. He bumped his head on two separate branches, flipped over completely, and lost his direction. He panicked, flailing his arms and legs and reaching out to grab any stem that he could get a hold of and that would hold him. He missed each time. The breeze changed course and sent him spiraling downward.

"Help!" Nut cried out, but no one heard him.

Meanwhile, ahead of him Leaf and Twig coursed easily through the myriad of branches, mosses, vines, stems and leaves of the giant tree. They hurdled the gnarls (the large knots on branches), zoomed through the breaks (gaps between branches), sling slung (swinging on vines) through the V's (where branches meet the trunk), and caught air (free floating up from level to level), as they sped onward, upward and downward toward school.

They weren't the only ones running late for class. Shady and his cohorts Rake and Stump were slowly walking along a back road branch looking to hurt anything they could find. They would usually tear off weak leaves from young stems, shoot mush-berries with slingshots at unwary insects, and cut vines with sharp sticks. They weren't generally nice to nature (or anyone else) and today wasn't any different. Rake was presently targeting in on a tri-colored butterfly that had landed on the prettiest blue moss-flower, when Shady suddenly grabbed his wrist.

"What?" Rake chirped, obviously annoyed by the intrusion. He was taller and stronger than Shady, and always thought of himself as smarter. "I had a great shot at that…"

"Shhh!" Shady interrupted. "Listen."

"I don't hear nothin'!" Stump bellowed.

"Quiet, you toad," Shady said and slapped the big fellow on the side of his head.

"Ouch! Why did you…"

"There!" Shady suddenly pointed up and to the left. "Someone's coming fast and I bet I know who."

"My dad?" Stump said softly, while rubbing his head.

"Leaf!" Rake said, matter-of-factly. "And that irritating little shrub-bucket Twig, too."

Stump wanted to mention Nut, but Shady grabbed him and pulled him behind a branch before he had a chance to speak. Shady knelt down behind some moss and readied his slingshot. Rake took aim with his sling,

too. Stump didn't have one. He could never quite figure out how to work it without smacking his own hand.

"Steady, Rake," Shady commanded. "Don't fire until they get close."

"This is gonna hurt so good," Rake said snidely.

"I wish I could see," said Stump from behind the branch.

"Shhh!" Shady and Rake hushed.

A few levels up and to the left, Leaf was a mere spider's leg ahead of Twig as they hurdled a gnarl, plowed through a V and were set to catch some air. A few more steps, then a leap, and they'd be floating right into the ambush set below them.

"Weeehaaaa!" Twig yelled. "Get ready to launch!"

"Watch me tuck and dive straight to school!" said Leaf.

"Me, too," added Twig.

As Leaf and Twig leapt from the branch, Shady and Rake rose up to fire, when out of the blue—more like out of the green—Nut came hurtling through the branches like a limb that had been blown off a tree by a hurricane.

"Watch ooooout!" Nut screamed, plowing right between Shady and Rake and heading downward. The two barely managed to catch their footing when Leaf and Twig whisked through and bumped them enough to send them spinning off their ambush perch and falling to the branches below.

"What were Shady and Rake doing?" Twig asked, as he and Leaf continued their descent.

"I don't know, but we knocked them down at least four levels," Leaf said laughing.

It was then the boys glanced ahead to see Nut, who had a look of sheer horror in his eyes. He was holding on to a tiny stem and swinging in the air. They landed next to him and helped him to his feet.

"How'd you get here so fast?" Twig asked, looking back up into the higher branches.

Nut thought for a second, looked back up at the way he had come, and said, "I, um, I guess I tripped." The boys broke out laughing and even Nut had to chuckle at himself as they headed off to school.

Slightly bruised and ego-battered, Shady and Rake fumed while hanging precariously from vines they had grabbed to stop their fall.

"I'm gonna get that Twig!" Rake said, while rubbing his knee. "I rammed my leg on that V we passed."

"Oh, they'll pay, all right," Shady said. "Wait until today's sailing race, Rake. We'll sink those pests like a…" His words were cut short as Stump came busting through the vines.

"I'll save you guys!" Stump yelled.

"No, Stump, no!!!" said Shady. But it was too late. Stump careened into them like a boulder through a patch of daisies. They lost their grip on the vines and the three of them fell off even further into the branches below.

CHAPTER TWO

HISTORY

As Leaf, Twig, and Nut floated down toward school they could see the other kids lining up to go inside their classes. The classrooms were roomy arbors situated on the grand east side educational branch, and were constructed of stick beams covered with vines and regular leaves. There was the "Acorn" class of preschoolers; the "Sprig" class for kindergarteners; the "Sprout - One's, Two's and Three's" classes of first through third grades; the "Stem" class of fourth graders; the "Shoot" class of fifth graders and, finally, their class—called the "Blooms" of sixth graders. The boys didn't like the name "Blooms," but the girls did, especially Garland.

If there was ever a girl that Leaf liked, it was Garland. He thought she was the greatest. She could run, float, flip, swim, shoot arrows, sword fight, sail, and do anything else as well as any other student in their class. With the exception of sailing class and swordplay, Garland was Leaf's favorite reason to go to school, even if she did like the name "Blooms."

School began with history, reading and writing in the morning, a nice long lunch break, and then sword fighting, archery, swimming, and finally, sailing in the afternoon. As the boys sat down in their bark desks for history class, Nut practiced his rhyme.

"Hardy Hardknot we hardly knew, Timber Thickroot was…"

"Thickbranch, Nut," Twig corrected. "Timber Thickbranch was number two."

"I'll never get it right," Nut whined. "There's too many of them."

"All right," announced Mrs. Perchwell, their teacher. "Who knows what today is?"

"Tuesday!" announced Shady, as he burst through the door with Rake and Stump close behind. He stared hard at Leaf and said, "Today is sink or sail Tuesday."

"It may be Tuesday, Master Shady Figthorn," said Mrs. Perchwell. "But whether you sink or sail during today's sailing race, you will still be here after school for detention since you strolled in late." She pointed at Rake and Stump. "And you two also, Mr. Rake Raven and Mr. Stumply Nettletick."

The rest of the class giggled. They always giggled when Mrs. Perchwell said Stump's name, and since he was often in trouble, they giggled a lot.

"All right, now children," she continued. "Since this is a history class, who can tell me what is significant about today, April twelfth?"

The kids were silent and looked around at each other. Leaf felt that he should know the answer, but it wasn't coming. Twig raised his hand.

"Yes, Master Twigford?"

"Is today the day that Anson the Antthumper thumped the two ant generals at the Battle of Rabbit's Run?"

Mrs. Perchwell smiled brightly and she shook her head up and down.

"Why…..no," she said. "But at least that shows you know about our history with the ants. There has always been bad blood between us and those ants. Generations have passed, and we still have to be vigilant, so it's never a bad time to discuss the dangers of ants." She turned to pull down a chart hanging from the ceiling. The class moaned, because they knew she would say…"Let's recite the 'Triple-A's'!"

The class read together, and not a few of them were a little bored doing it, since they had been reciting the list from the time they were "Acorns" in pre-school.

"The Triple-A's! Ant - Awareness - Alert."

"Number One – Where there's one, there's more to come."

"Number Two – Stop your play and run away."

"Number Three – If you're trapped lay down real flat. Rug out!"

The kids always yelled, "Rug out!" when they recited number three. It was slang for, "lay flat like a rug and become like a regular fallen leaf."

"Number Four - Do your best to warn the rest."

"Number Five – Don't lead them here, get free and clear."

"Number Six – Throw a berry, make them merry."

"Number Seven – Never fight in dark of night."

"Or you just might…get a bite!" Shady yelled and made the class laugh. Garland turned and smiled at Shady. Leaf saw him wink back at her and he didn't like it at all. He wanted to think of a funny rhyme but couldn't do it fast enough.

"Number Eight – If you get bit, you have to spit." (Some of the class still giggled at the thought of spitting, even though everyone knew that the only thing that could quickly relieve an ant bite was leaf spit.)

"Number Nine – Cut the head, make them dead." And all the boys said, "Yeah!"

"Number Ten – For tree and land, together stand."

"Very good, class," said Mrs. Perchwell, as she tugged the string on the chart to make it roll back up. "Moving back to history, what is significant about today?"

Garland's hand shot up. She knew the answer but waited for the Triple A's to end.

"Yes, Miss Garland Green?"

"April twelfth of last year is the day that Leaf's father and the rest of the sailors set sail for Lands Unknown," she said matter-of-factly.

"Why yes, it is," said Mrs. Perchwell. "Yes, it is." She glanced at Leaf, but he wasn't looking. He was too embarrassed for not knowing the answer. Shady raised his hand, but didn't wait to be called on.

"His father wouldn't make it to 'Lands Unknown' if it wasn't for the 'rest of the sailors,'" chimed Shady. "It's on the sweaty backs of the rowers and the calloused hands of the sail men that our great heroes of old and new made history." He directed the last word toward Mrs. Perchwell.

Most of the class seemed to agree with Shady and murmured their approval, since many, like Shady, were the children of sailors. Even Garland nodded her head in agreement. Twig and Nut looked to Leaf, who raised himself in his seat.

"If it wasn't for the great heroes and visionaries of old and new," said Leaf, "the rowers would still have sweaty backs and the sail men's hands would still have calluses, only they'd be called caterpillar herders and farmers instead of explorers."

Some of the students took offense and "booed" while others brightened up and applauded. Leaf stood and addressed the class.

"They are all heroes and explorers and they work together as a team. There is a chart man, and a cook, and a lookout, and bailers, and rowers, and sail men, and a captain who leads them, but they are all explorers seeking lands that will one day, hopefully, become known. One day our forest won't have any trees, and we had better know where we are going before the inevitable happens."

Most of the students moaned, knowing that Leaf was bringing up a subject that no one agreed with.

"Hogwash!" cried Shady. "Here we go again, with, 'The trees are disappearing, the trees are disappearing!' Come on, Leaf, no one else believes this fairytale except you and your hero father. Look around us. We don't see anything but trees."

Most of the class laughed and began to talk at the same time. It seemed they all thought Leaf had lost his mind…again. Rake shot a nasty smile at Twig, who sat staring at the floor. Nut put his head on his desk. Leaf headed for the door.

"All right, class, quiet down and get ready for the Scroll Exam," said Mrs. Perchwell, who then noticed Leaf leaving. "Where do you think you are going? Leaf! Come back here, Master Eric's son!" But Leaf ignored her and kept on walking.

CHAPTER THREE
SHOW AND TELL

Leaf didn't get very far. Principal Oakreach was in the hallway when Leaf exited his classroom.

"Leaving a little early, are we?"

"Yes, sir," Leaf admitted. His head was lowered and a tear rolled down his cheek.

"Don't feel well, Leaf?"

"No, sir. May I go home?"

"What's the matter, son?"

The principal put his arm around Leaf's shoulder and led him to his office. Leaf liked Principal Oakreach and had at many times been invited to his office for nectar shakes and honey cakes. "Shakes-n-Cakes" was the principal's way of rewarding the best students. Most times they would play games, like "Beetle Race," or "Thorn Toss," but every so often the principal would strum a spider-weave and sing songs that reminded Leaf of the heroes of old.

Alone I soared through bough and beam
And set my course by sun and breeze
In time to rise above the heights
Touching briefly starry lights

And called upon the roots so deep
Don't mourn for me but should you weep
For leaves I've passed along the way
Who choose to sleep both night and day
Oh forest arm and woodland band
Undo your hold release your hand
For though I'm born of earth and rains
Of golden beams and green-spring veins
I found myself ere drawn to be
By creek by brook by winding stream
The freest leaf ne'er bound of tree
At last at home upon the sea

Leaf would get lost in the words, and imagine soaring through the upper branches of trees and then sailing the wide-open ocean. His heart raced as he daydreamed, though he suspected it could also be a result of the Shakes-n-Cakes.

As the two sat down, Leaf explained what happened in class. Principal Oakreach wasn't a stranger to Leaf's concern with a dwindling forest, as he had often heard Leaf's father voice the same thoughts at the Tree Council meetings. Principal Oakreach had been on the council for a long time.

As Leaf spoke, the principal nodded his head with understanding and stood up to remove a wooden cylindrical container from his bookshelf. He pulled out the contents and laid them on the table. Maps—some of them very old.

"Take a look at these, Leaf, and tell me what you see."

The principal spread one out, which was tiny compared to the rest.

Leaf scanned the crude drawing and immediately picked out their tree in the center of the map, a huge oak, which dominated its domain. Surrounding it were scores of trees, along with the hollows and glens that made up most of the land that Leaf already knew. There were creeks and

brooks and streams that led to the river, and there were trails that led deeper into the forest. Leaf noticed the creek that ran around the tree from its eastern side and the small hill that rose on the west and south. Though trees were everywhere, the hill had what looked to be an X marked on it.

"What is the X for?" asked Leaf.

"That's not an X, young Eric's son. Those are crossed swords, where Anson the Antthumper fought and won the Battle of Rabbit's Run. Not a bad looking drawing for a warrior, eh?"

"He made this map?" Leaf asked, astonished.

"He certainly did. He had more talents than simply ant thumping."

The principal unrolled a second map. It was bigger than the first and was much more intricately drawn. In fact, it was beautiful.

"Wow!" Leaf exclaimed. "It's incredible! It's a work of art."

The map covered roughly the same area as the first, but it had much more detail. Leaf saw that the tree was drawn level by level, complete with gnarls and V's. From there the map branched out, as if every tree, vine, bush, hedge, and thicket were accounted. Every boulder, every rock, every berry patch, and every floral glade could be seen. There were rabbits hopping near their holes, deer foraging on trails, and squirrels leaping through the trees. There were butterflies and bees and every type of bird found in the forest.

Leaf followed the course of the creek as it wound around the first easterly bend and joined the northern stream to eventually become the river that leads to the bay. The map showed every twist and turn, every sandbar, every connecting creek and every tree-bridge that spanned the water along the way.

"Who drew this?" Leaf asked.

"This is the map of my great-grandfather, Oakley the Reacher."

Leaf suddenly realized the significance of Principal Oakreach's name.

"You're the great explorer's great-grandson?" Leaf asked in amazement.

Principal Outreach bowed. "At your service. As a young boy, about your age, I had the honor of hearing him speak of his travels. Unfortunately for your ears, as an old man, I have the inclination to sing his songs."

Leaf wanted to tell the principal how much he enjoyed the songs, but at that moment he was too lost in his thoughts to say anything. His mind swirled with visions of adventure and discovery, of danger and triumph, and of exploring strange lands that no one had ever seen.

"I want to go!" he blurted out.

"Go where?" the principal asked.

"On adventures, where no one has gone, and map out the…"

Leaf suddenly stopped, a pained look on his face.

"What's the matter?" asked Principal Oakreach.

"I can't draw." Leaf said with a cry in his voice.

The principal laughed long and loud until his eyes watered and he had to wipe them with his hands. He took out the third map.

"That's okay, young Eric's son," he said still laughing. "Neither could your grandfather."

The principal showed Leaf the third map, which was newer than the other two, but was so roughly drawn that Leaf couldn't tell what it was supposed to depict.

"Your grandfather, Erin the Bold, drew this. See the big stick with the billowy top?" the principal asked.

"Yes, sir."

"That's our tree," the principal assured.

"You're kidding," Leaf said. But sure enough, Leaf could somehow tell that what looked like a dandelion after the seed pods had mushroomed was meant to be the tree. Leaf chuckled.

"Grandpa Erin wasn't the best artist, was he?"

"No, but he was able enough to get the job done. See, this line here is the creek that runs around the tree and the thicker line is where the northern stream and the creeks converge to form the river. The river runs down to the bay and that's where the Coastals live. Grandpa Erin was the first to get there. It was a very harrowing journey."

Leaf saw about fifty short square boxes and five long rectangles on land and what looked like longboats on the water. The area all around the Coastal settlement and all around the tree was shaded. The principal spoke before Leaf could ask.

"The shaded-in area all around is the forest."

Leaf looked at the map and saw that it was a very small area where the Coastals lived and that the forest was very large in comparison. The principal pointed to the other two maps.

"The forest is the same in each map, Leaf. This is proof from generations ago to the recent generation of your grandfather, that our home isn't going anywhere. They may cut down a few trees here and there, but we are in no danger. Our forest is grand!"

CHAPTER FOUR

SPLISH SPLASH

By the time Leaf left the principal's office, the rest of the students were eating lunch on the courtyard branch. Leaf wasn't hungry. His mind was filled with too many thoughts. He thought about his father and wondered how much longer he would be out to sea. It had been a year since the ship had sailed and that was by far the longest the men had ever been gone. Leaf remembered the last words his father said to him before hugging his mom and setting off.

"I'm taking them out as far as we can go," he'd said. "We have to break free of our coastlines and head to new lands yet unknown. We don't have long before our forest is gone."

The words seemed empty now. It was as if his father was fighting battles against an enemy that didn't exist. Leaf felt all at once foolish for believing his father and remorse for not believing. It was as if he had betrayed his father's trust.

"Are you going to eat your pecan soup?" Twig asked Leaf.

Leaf stared off into the distance of the courtyard where the younger kids who had finished eating were beginning to run around and play. Leaf, Twig and Nut sat at a small table away from the other students of their class.

"I don't think he heard you, Twig," said Nut. "I have dibs on his berry muffin!"

Twig and Nut both reached for Leaf's food, but received lightning-fast knocks on their knuckles from Leaf's spoon.

"Ow!" They both cried out.

"Y… y…you didn't have to do that," Nut whined.

Twig rubbed his hand and looked at Leaf, who returned to staring into the distance.

"So, are you going to eat your pecan soup?" Twig asked again.

"No, you can have it," Leaf said. Twig took the soup and Nut reached for the muffin but took another knock on the knuckle.

"Ow!"

Before Nut could say anything, three shadows came from behind the boys to block the midday sun around their table. Shady, Rake and Stump stood with their hands on their hips.

"Pretty fast with that spoon, there, Tree-Counter," Shady teased. "I hope you're as fast with an oar this afternoon."

Rake pointed at Twig.

"You're going swimming, '*Master*' Twigford," Rake said with an evil grin.

Stump pointed at Nut.

"Um, ah….yeah," Stump mumbled, not knowing what to say.

Normally, the boys would ignore the three troublemakers. Twig would say something like, "Did you hear something, Leaf?" and Leaf would respond, "No, but I smell something. Hey, Nut, did you step in a pile of moose pudding?" Nut would look at his feet, not getting the joke, but the effect usually worked and they would ignore the confrontation.

But the boys didn't let it go this time. Leaf suddenly jumped up from his seat to stand toe to toe with Shady. Twig rose up too, but he had a different idea. Faster than a fish can say "splish-splash" Twig threw the pecan soup, bowl and all, into Rake's face.

"Take a bird bath in that, Rake Raven!" Twig shouted and tackled Rake to the ground. When Shady turned to help Rake, Leaf grabbed him with one hand and snatched a vine with the other. He swung Shady out and over the courtyard branch and let go. Shady went sailing. He attempted to flip up but a breeze sent him spinning downward.

"I'm gonna get youuuuuuuuu!" was all Leaf could hear as Shady slipped out of sight.

Leaf turned to see Twig on top of Rake as they wrestled. Stump bent over to grab Twig, but Nut climbed up onto his chair, then the table, and jumped on Stump's back, making him fall on top of the two wrestlers. Twig and Rake both groaned under the weight and quit their fight.

As a crowd of kids from all the classes gathered around, Mrs. Perchwell and Principal Oakreach ran in to break it up. Garland pushed her way through the throng as well.

"That's enough!" Mrs. Perchwell screamed. And so it was. As Nut slid off of Stump, Principal Oakreach lifted Stump from on top of Twig and Rake. Both of the boys moaned in relief.

"No racing for you four boys today!" the principal said. He looked at Leaf, who was off to the side by the edge of the branch. "Where's Master Figthorn, Leaf? I can't believe you two weren't involved in this." Leaf simply shrugged his shoulders and peered over the side of the branch.

"I guess he's floating around here somewhere."

CHAPTER FIVE
OAR NOT

As Twig, Nut, Rake, and Stump were being herded off to the office by Principal Oakreach, and as the other children made their way to their classes, Garland walked with Leaf to their fencing class.

There was a turmoil brewing inside her, and she couldn't quite get a grasp on where the unsettling feeling was coming from or how to handle it. She cared about Leaf and worried that maybe he didn't care enough about himself. *He's been saying and doing childish things and maybe that is why I feel this way,* she thought. *I'm growing up, and he's still acting like a kid.* She tried to shake it off, but for some reason she felt responsible to help him. There were words she wanted to say, feelings she wanted to convey, but maybe this wasn't the time.

"What are you going to do without a crew?" she asked. "You and Shady are going to have a rough time sailing solo."

"I'll still beat him," Leaf said with vinegar in his voice, and his self-centered tone sent a shiver down Garland's stalk. She couldn't hold back any more.

"I wasn't only talking about him, you know? There *are* six *other* boats to contend with. Look, Leaf, I don't know what it is between you and him, and I really don't care. The main thing is there's a lot more going on around you than your private little war with Shady Figthorn. Twig and Nut admire you and I'll bet that fight today had something to do with their need to stand up for you. You're going to be in a position of leadership someday and you have to think about the future and well-being of the entire Colony. Don't you know that your actions and your words can have an effect on other leaves, and when you lose sight of everything else and focus on Shady or on disappearing trees, then you're missing the forest for the trees. And I can't...."

Garland choked out the last words with a cry. Leaf stood dumbfounded, not knowing what to say. He wanted to defend himself and shout, *I do care about the Colony; I thought the trees really were disappearing;* or *Shady's a bug who's always picking fights,* but the only thing he could say was, "I'm sorry."

He tried to put his arm around her, but she shrugged it off and ran inside the nearest classroom.

Their swimming and archery classes had been canceled for the day because of the race preparations, but they did manage to get in a short fencing class. Mr. Frostcone, the fencing instructor, stood at attention as the students filed into the duel yard, a thorny-thicket enclosed wall and ceiling arena, away from the younger students' classrooms. It was a dangerous instructional area, but it was designed that way on purpose. Mr. Frostcone wanted his classes to have respect and to be on edge. The thorns were a perfect touch.

Mr. Frostcone was a very proud and stern man, and he rattled off the day's exercises of thrusting and parrying as if he were speaking to a classroom of soldiers. He had been training soldiers up until the day that Leaf's father decided that shipbuilding was a more important venture than military training. With the military all but disbanded, Mr. Frostcone found the only place his services were needed—elementary school. He was not a happy man.

As he spoke, Leaf, who normally loved fencing, was not paying attention. He was preoccupied by the day's events and the thought of the upcoming race. Mr. Frostcone noticed, and since he was a bit put off already by the scheduling change for a "puddle push," as he called the boat race, he was doubly unhappy to see Leaf's attention wandering. It didn't help that Leaf was Eric's son.

"En garde!" Mr. Frostcone shouted, leveling his sword at Leaf. Leaf stood there in shock, his sword pointed to the ground. Everyone in the class gasped, except Shady, who smiled and secretly wished the teacher would skewer Leaf to a rotten branch. No one knew what to expect since the teacher had never done anything like that before. Garland cried out.

"What are you doing, Mr. Frostcone?" she asked.

"If this young man doesn't pay attention in my class, he might get stung," the teacher answered and stabbed toward Leaf. "En garde, now!"

The teacher thrust at Leaf, who parried to the right, the tip barely missing Leaf's chest. The thunk of the two sharp wooden swords meeting echoed off the thorny thicket of the duel yard and widened every eye in the place, including Leaf's. The two circled each other, with Leaf mainly trying to get away. The teacher feinted low and came in high to Leaf's neck, but Leaf ducked and leapt to the right, bringing his sword up in time to knock the teacher's attack away. The rest of the students scrambled out of their path, pushing and knocking into each other. Some even ran into the thicket thorns and cut themselves, but Mr. Frostcone didn't notice or care.

"It's a cruel world out there, Master Eric's son," the teacher warned. "It's a very cruel world and you had better be ready for it!" He sprang at Leaf and thrust toward Leaf's stomach, but wasn't quick enough as Leaf flipped backward and away, brushing against the thorns to his back as he landed on his feet. The thorns gave him an idea and he quickly scanned the roof of the arena for the perfect place to put his plan into action.

As the teacher circled to Leaf's left, Leaf ran the opposite way, caught air, and grabbed a stem of a thicket that hung down from the roof. As the roof was too high to reach from the ground, the only course for Mr. Frostcone to take was to catch air himself and join Leaf on the ceiling. But it's not easy to catch air and sword fight at the same time. Arms are necessary to propel one's self off the ground. As Mr. Frostcone took off, Leaf waited for him to get close and then quickly dropped. He spun behind and under him and then zoomed back up, grabbing and pushing the teacher into the thorny roof where he stuck like bark to a new sapling. His sword fell with a thud to the ground.

Mr. Frostcone screamed, his body pierced in twenty places by the thorns. Leaf floated back down and picked up the sword.

"Someone get me down!" the teacher shouted.

"If I get you down, will you promise not to attack me anymore?" Leaf asked.

"Yes. Get me down!"

And with that, Leaf helped him down and class was dismissed. Mr. Frostcone went to the infirmary, and everyone but Shady congratulated Leaf on surviving the assault.

Later that afternoon the entire school (minus Twig, Nut, Rake, Stump and Mr. Frostcone) gathered at the docks for the sailing races. Each class had their individual events, including the Acorns who—though they weren't allowed in the water—raced their tiny, homemade bark boats to a chorus of rooters from the pier.

The Sprigs' two boats were big safety canoes with outriggers on the sides. Two teams of ten manned each one, with the canoes harnessed in the back by a rope much longer than the race course. No one wanted a Sprig to go too far down the creek.

The Sprouts were the first class to be allowed to race a three-person boat, though only with oars—no sails were allowed at the Sprouts' level. The Stems and Shoots used both sails and oars, but only competed on the short course of fifty meters.

As each class raced, the onlookers went wild, cheering for friends, or older brothers or younger sisters, or anyone who was competing. Even though there were lots of classes to cheer for, more and more eyes were checking on the Blooms, who were getting their boats ready far behind the starting line. Theirs was the big race—the last one for the class—and the one that everyone wanted to eventually win.

There were supposed to be six teams of three each. Today was an exception as Leaf and Shady manned their boats alone. Leaf's boat was named the *Red* in honor of his father Eric the Red Leaf. Shady's boat, the *Purple Bruiser*, wasn't named in honor of anyone.

Garland and her crew, Misty Boggs and Heather Fern, were preparing their racer, the *Gar Green*, named in honor of Garland's father, who was a famous shipbuilder. He had designed and built the *Flying Vine* that Leaf's father was sailing now. It was the fastest and sleekest ship ever built in the history of the Colony.

The other boats were named the *Yellow Fin,* the *Bob Brown,* and the *White Wasp.* All the crews wore their ship's colors and had flags to match their theme. Leaf's flag was a red leaf. Shady's was a fist.

Mrs. Perchwell blew her cone whistle to get everyone's attention. She stood on a podium with the other teachers, and behind them were the trophies. The biggest trophy was for the Blooms. It was a replica of the *Flying Vine* and it had a place for the names of the crew members and for the name of their boat.

"Okay, everyone, hush now," she said as the Acorns, Sprigs, Sprouts, Stems and Shoots gathered around. "I can't remember a year when we've had such beautiful weather and so many wonderful boats. You racers who have finished already have given us all a magnificent show today."

With that, there was an outburst of applause and many pats on the back.

"But now, you younger boys and girls, it is my pleasure to introduce to you the participants of the main event. This is the longest and toughest race you will ever witness, and in the years to come, it might be you who gets to the finish line first."

Everyone applauded and cheered. Leaf, who was in the first position because he had drawn a number one out of the bag, glanced to his left at the other boats. Luckily, he thought, Shady was at the far end. Garland was next to Leaf, and then the White, Yellow, and Brown teams accordingly.

"First of all, you will notice that two of the teams are flying solo today. Let that be a warning to you. If you break the rules you will miss out on even the most important functions. Now, in the first position we have the *Red,* captained and manned today by Leaf, Eric's son!"

The crowd applauded loudly as all the younger kids thought highly of Leaf, not in the least for being the grandson of Erin the Bold Leaf and the son of Eric the Red Leaf.

"Next, is Garland Green captaining the *Gar Green* named in honor of…"

As Mrs. Perchwell spoke, Leaf became lost in thought. He saw himself flying down the creek, his boat barely touching the water and then taking off like the white seabirds his father told him about. Leaf soared through the trees in his boat and mapped out lands unknown. He was about to conquer an army of flying red fire ants when Mrs. Perchwell's words snapped him out of his daydream.

"Now, when I blow my whistle," Mrs. Perchwell said, addressing the racers, "you will row to the end of Tree Creek, turn at the marker right before the junction of the Northern Branch and sail back again to the starting point. Are there any questions?"

No one said a word—not even Shady, who was busy making sure his sail was ready to hoist. Leaf considered the course, how he was going to row, maneuver at the marker, set sail, and make it back again. It was going to be tough doing it alone but he envisioned the steps he needed to take to make it work.

"Are you ready?" Mrs. Perchwell yelled. All of the children screamed and cheered. "Here we go! On your marks! Get set!" TWEEEEEEEEEEEET! The whistle sounded, and off they went.

Leaf and Shady fell behind almost immediately as the three-man crews out-oared them.

Garland looked back at Leaf and yelled, "Told you!" The girls giggled

to themselves but only for a moment as the Brown and Yellow teams took the lead. As the other boats pulled ahead, Leaf and Shady became caught in their wakes and drifted closer and closer to the middle of the course. Soon the two were side by side, their oars banging up against one another.

"Move away!" Leaf yelled.

"You move!" Shady screamed back.

Leaf put down one oar to use the other to push Shady's boat away from his own. Shady had the idea too and knocked Leaf's oar away. Pretty soon they both stood up and began "sword" fighting with oars. Leaf caught Shady in the armpit and pushed. Shady fell back and into the water; Leaf couldn't stop his momentum and fell forward into the water as well.

They might have kept on fighting in the water if wasn't for the unexpected sound the whole Colony had been waiting to hear for some time—three conch-shell blasts that signaled the return of the *Flying Vine*! Leaf's father and the crew had returned!

CHAPTER SIX
STICKS, LINES, AND BOXES

It didn't take long for everyone to make their way to the docks. Young and old, male and female dropped what they were doing and floated down or came running from every part of the tree. Leaf's mom, who had been busy making meals for the elderly men of the Old Sailor's Club, came floating down with Leaf's little sister, Flower. Flower was only eleven-months old, and had never seen her father.

"Hi, Mom!" Leaf called from the dock.

"Hi, honey," she called back as she landed next to him. "How was the…" She wanted to ask him about the race, but then noticed he was dripping wet. "What happened to you?"

"Oh, I started off okay, but then…" His words were cut short as his father came leaping off of the ship to run and embrace his mom. Leaf watched them embrace each other, and thought the hug was tighter than a caterpillar's cocoon. Then his father took Flower in his arms and kissed her. He looked her over from head to toe, hugged her again and then looked to Leaf.

"It's so good to be home," he said. "How are you, Son….besides wet? I pushed the crew to make it back today for the sailing races. I guess today was the swimming races."

They all laughed.

"I'm fine, Dad. I really missed you." Leaf thought about all the things he wanted to ask his dad. How was the journey? How far did you go? Did you find a new land? What about the trees? Before he could ask, his father turned his attention to his mom and then the ship.

"I have to go back and make sure everything is unloaded, dear," Eric said.

"I know," she said. "I have to make sure a hot bath is ready for you when you come home. You stink, Captain."

"Stink!" Flower said, and they all laughed again.

Later that night, Leaf's father sat in his comfortable bark-a-lounger holding a sleeping Flower and sipping a cup of hot maple tea. Leaf's mom relaxed in her chair and Leaf sat on the floor playing with their pet spider, Stretch. Stretch was a tiny daddy longlegs who liked to walk from hand to hand, running up one of Leaf's shoulders, and then down the other. He could do it for as long as Leaf could stand the tickle.

"All right, Stretch, that's enough," Leaf squealed. "Sit." Stretch plopped down in Leaf's lap and waited for him to pet his tiny head. Leaf didn't let him wait long. Stretch splayed all eight of his legs out to the sides in complete relaxation.

"How about playing a song, Dad?" Leaf asked.

"Oh, it's been a long time. What should I play?"

Eric knew what Leaf would say. He always requested the same song.

"Oh Sail Along With Me!" Leaf said.

Eric set down his mug and stretched his arms. Leaf's mom stood up and took little Flower from his lap, and carried her off to the crib in her bedroom. Eric picked up his spider-weave from the side of his chair and began strumming the happy melody. His voice wasn't very pretty, but he caught every nuance of the chorus.

Oh sail along with me

Through the thickest trees

Down the creek

And up the stream

Oh sail along with me

Leaf sang harmony to the chorus as best he could, but his mom really nailed the part as she hurried back into the room. Eric started the first verse.

We sailed away one April day

And rowed with all our might

We didn't get too far you see

The ropes still held us tight

The three laughed loudly, and then Leaf's mom sang the second verse.

The women ran to kiss the men

On head and cheek and lip

And asked, how did your journey fare

Why such a lengthy trip

Oh sail along with me

Through the thickest trees

Down the creek

And up the stream

Oh sail along with me

As usual, Leaf sang the next verse.

The boys and girls all had a plan

To stow away that night

But as they snuck onto the dock

The ship was not in sight

Leaf's mom and dad sang the last verse.

And far across the waters deep

They heard their moms and dads

We'll be home in the morning dears
Now get yourselves to bed
Oh sail along with me
Through the thickest trees
Down the creek
And up the stream
Oh sail along with me

The three laughed loudly and then hushed themselves so as not to wake Flower. They giggled at their silliness and Leaf's mom kissed both of them on their heads. Eric set down the spider-weave and took a sip from his mug.

"I guess I should tell you about the adventures we had, eh, Son?"

"Yes, please!" Leaf begged.

Eric took a deep breath and exhaled slowly. He thought of the things that Leaf should know concerning the voyage and also about the things he shouldn't know—at least not until he was older. There were a few things he might even have to spare Leaf's mother from learning. The less she knew, the less she might worry. Then, he realized, she would worry anyway, and regarding Leaf, he might as well tell him, too. It would be better for them to hear it from him than finding out from someone else. Thicket Figthorn was sure to tell his son Shady everything. So Eric decided he would tell them the whole story, too.

"We set sail early on April 12th of last year," he began. "As you remember, the weather was pretty cold for April."

"It snowed during our races," Leaf said.

"Yes, it must have. It snowed on us about halfway down to the bay. That's probably why we didn't see any ant patrols on the cross-logs spanning the creek. They usually post a few guards there, too, and we have to, um, *remove* them before they see the ship."

Leaf giggled at the way his father said "remove them." He knew what he meant. Mom knew, too, and glared at Leaf for giggling.

"So, even though it was cold, it took the usual six days to get to the bay," Eric continued. "I put the ship ashore north of the Coastals so I could scout out the extent of their settlements. That's when I had the first run-in with Thicket Figthorn."

"Again?" Leaf's mom asked.

"It's something every time, hon," Eric said. "He's always trying to undermine my authority. He doesn't understand that not only should we keep our maps up-to-date, but we need to know how close the Coastals are coming to our part of the forest. One day they'll be chopping down our tree, I know it."

With that, Leaf began squirming in his chair so much that it disturbed Stretch's rest. The spider gave Leaf an annoyed look, but Leaf didn't notice. Leaf's mom noticed, though, and more than that.

"What is it, Leaf?" she asked. "You have a very strange look on your face."

Leaf stiffened and straightened himself where he sat. He didn't want them to know how he felt, but he looked like a bear cub who had learned the pointed truth that the fuzzy little toy he wanted to play with was actually a porcupine.

Leaf hesitated. It took a concerned look from his father to convince him to say what was on his mind. "Principal Oakreach showed me Grandpa Erin's map, and also the maps made before him."

"Oh, that was nice," his mom said. "He's such a thoughtful man, isn't he, Eric?"

"Yes," Eric said with little enthusiasm, knowing what was coming. Oakley Oakreach had shown the maps to the Tree Council on more than one occasion—especially since Eric had begun to voice his concerns about the Coastals. He leaned forward in his chair toward Leaf. "So, Son, was there any difference in the tree lines?"

Leaf realized his father knew about the maps. "No, Dad, there wasn't," he answered sadly. "They looked the same from generation to generation."

Eric leaned back in his chair and sighed. Leaf felt horrible. It was as if he had betrayed his father and sided with someone else—everyone else. The thought that he had sided with Thicket and Shady Figthorn made him feel even worse.

"I'm sorry, Dad."

Eric grinned from ear to ear and even chuckled a bit.

"Sorry for what, Son? You have nothing to be sorry about."

"Yes, I do. I believed you, and now….now I don't know." He bowed his head and tears fell down his cheek.

Leaf's mom sighed and looked to Eric to fix the situation. Eric rose from his chair and sat down next to Leaf. He pulled a rolled-up piece of paper from his travel sack.

"Want to see the *newest* map?" Eric said with a smile on his face.

Leaf looked up and wiped the tears from his eyes. He saw his father's smile and wondered what could make his father so happy at a moment like this. They looked at each other without moving.

"Well?" Eric said.

"Yes," Leaf blurted out. "Yes, please show me!"

Eric unrolled the map and Leaf giggled. Leaf's mom sat down on the floor with them and looked at the drawing, too.

"What's so funny?" she asked.

"Dad draws like Grandpa Erin, with sticks and lines and boxes."

They laughed, and Eric had to nod his head in agreement.

"Your grandpa taught me everything I know," he chuckled. "And one thing I know for sure is that the Coastals are getting closer."

Leaf studied his father's drawing. It was a crude and hurriedly drawn map, but Leaf knew how to read it since he'd already seen his grandfather's.

"The big dandelion is our tree," Leaf said with a chuckle and began tracing the rest with his finger. "Here's the creek running over to meet the Northern Branch, and this is the river going down to the bay. The Coastal settlement is…."

Leaf paused and stared at his father with a look of shock.

"Dad! The Coastals have doubled in size and…."

Leaf paused again.

"Oh, my!" he exclaimed.

"What is it?" Leaf's mom asked.

Eric sat still with a jumble of emotions. On the one hand he was very proud of his son, who could not only read the map but could understand its importance. On the other hand, he was very concerned for the safety of the Colony.

"There are roads, Mom. Dad went further inland than the other maps, and there are roads and other settlements connected, and….and….and they are everywhere! They are all around us and they are coming this way!"

Leaf suddenly leapt to his feet, which sent a startled Stretch flying through the air. Luckily he landed on Eric's cushioned bark-a-lounger. He sat there for a second with a look of shock on his face and then checked all of his legs to make sure none were hurt. He stared at Leaf with his tiny eyes bugging out as if to say, "What is wrong with you?"

"Good air, Stretch!" Leaf shouted. Stretch rolled his eyes and covered his head with his arms in disgust.

"Shhhh!" Leaf's mom implored. "Don't wake the baby."

CHAPTER SEVEN
MOVE

Leaf woke earlier than he usually did on a school day, and since he couldn't get back to sleep with all the excitement of the day before, and since school was cancelled due to the return of the *Flying Vine*, he decided to go out for a walk. Mom, Dad, Flower and even Stretch were still sleeping as he quietly opened the door and went outside onto the branch porch. Even though the sun was just beginning to rise, the air was already warmer than the days before. He thought about waking Twig and Nut, but changed his mind. A walk alone seemed like the thing to do, especially with all the events he felt he needed to contemplate. Dad's news was life changing.

"Don't tell anyone, Leaf," his father had said the night before. "No one else knows about this except you and your mother. You see, when I floated off to explore and map, I went alone. I was gone so long that Figthorn thought he could take over the ship and was about to sail off when I returned. I kept things quiet because we still needed to sail out to sea. We have to find a new home before we pack up and leave this one."

"Did you find it?" Leaf had asked. "Did you find a new home?"

"No," his father had said. "I didn't find it, but the Coastals did. They simply don't know what to do with it. I'm going to tell the council what I found out tomorrow afternoon."

Leaf walked along the main boulevard branch of the Colony thinking about his father's words. His mother had ushered him off to bed before his father could explain what he meant by "they don't know what to do with it."

It was quiet in the Colony. No one else was out yet, except an older couple walking their ladybug, and an annoying stray bark beetle that followed Leaf and clicked its razor-sharp jaws at him whenever he turned to look its way. Leaf wanted to amble and think, but he couldn't with the chew-happy pest creeping behind him.

They really should keep those things tied up, Leaf thought. They're a menace. The clicking was getting so bothersome that Leaf had had enough and decided to jump. He pretended to wave at someone across the branch, and when the beetle turned to see who he was waving at, Leaf leapt over the edge and out of sight.

"Finally," he said out loud as he floated through the lower levels, "peace and quiet."

He didn't know where he was going and felt like having the wind take him wherever it wanted. He picked up speed and decided to take a chance at zooming through the breaks to get to the other side of the tree. He hurdled two large gnarls and did a triple sling-slung to plow through the V. From there, he lost air through the next twenty levels until he could break free to the open space.

It was a perfect day for free-flying, with the breezes light and steady. He flipped and floated with ease in the open air doing figure-eights, back-sprawls, stalls, and toe-touches. He opened up his arms and deeply breathed in the fresh spring air.

"Ah," he exclaimed. "This is a gorgeous day!"

Leaf soon found himself on the western side of the tree where smaller bushes and trees dotted the ridge that protected their hamlet. He passed a large thicket of blackberry bushes that had only recently sprouted their shoots. He thought about the yummy-sweet berries that would be ready to eat in the summer, and the jams, jellies, pies and shakes his mom would make. Birds would flock there at dawn and dusk, and bees would swarm there, too. *Who could blame them,* Leaf thought.

As he passed into more open spaces, he looked down and spotted the rabbit burrows; although there weren't any crossed swords, he knew he had arrived at Rabbit's Run—the site of Anson the Antthumper's heroic victory. Leaf landed and then skedaddled (a combination of walking and flying at the same time, like a regular leaf blown along the ground by the wind). It wasn't easy walking there as the grass was high and the furrows deep, obviously dug by a gazillion rabbits.

"Right here is where the ant army was defeated," he said out loud from atop a tuft of grass. "I wonder what happened to the survivors."

"They went back to their queen," a voice called from behind him, which made Leaf almost jump right out of his veins. He quickly turned to see who it was, but there was no one there. He scanned from left to right but didn't see a soul. Feeling a bit nervous, he caught air high enough to rise above the grasses. There, in a hole of a furrow only a few feet away, was a furry creature with a pair of blinking eyes and a twitchy nose.

"You really scared me, Mr. Rabbit," Leaf said. "I thought you were…"

"Who are you calling Rabbit, Mister Talking Leaf?" said the furry creature. With that it sniffed, lifted its head and looked around before climbing half-way out of the hole.

"Oh, sorry, Mr. Groundhog," Leaf apologized. "I thought you were…"

"You do a lot of thinking, don't you, Thinking Leaf?" the groundhog interrupted. "But not enough, because I'm not a Mister. I'm a Miss!"

Leaf wasn't sure how he was supposed to know that, but started to apologize again anyway. The groundhog didn't care to wait.

"I'm not saying thinking's not good, you know, but sometimes thinking too much leaves one not moving. And these days you have to move."

"Why do you have to move?" Leaf asked, wondering if maybe he shouldn't ask since the groundhog seemed a bit pushy with her opinions. The groundhog moved completely out of the hole and edged closer to Leaf.

"The rabbits moved," the groundhog said, "but only because we moved and took over the rabbits' holes. We moved, but only because the mice moved and took over our holes. The mice moved, but only because the ants moved and took over the mices' holes. Is it mice, mice's, meece's, or mouse's? Anyway, the ants moved but only because the rains came and made the creeks change their courses, which flooded the ant holes. And the creeks moved their courses, but only because the trees moved."

"The trees moved?" Leaf said, not knowing what to make of that statement. "Trees don't move except when they're swaying back and forth in the…"

"They move when they are chopped down, Mister Talking-Without-Thinking-Leaf!" the groundhog said loudly and then nervously looked behind herself to see if anyone else had heard. She sniffed a few times, and then turned back to Leaf to speak a little softer.

"It's a chain reaction. You have one move, and then it's move, move, move, move, move," the groundhog said, and then sniffed again. Her twitchy face turned into a look of alarm.

"Uh, oh! Move!" And with that she quickly waddled backward into her hole till all Leaf could see was her eyes and nose once again.

"Move," the groundhog whispered.

Leaf looked around but didn't see or hear anything until it was almost too late. An army ant column was marching up a furrow only yards away.

The lead scouts had reached the crest but were looking low and to their sides instead of up to where Leaf hovered. Leaf immediately rugged out and fell to the ground. He laid down flat right next to the groundhog's hole. The groundhog twitched nervously.

"Oh, yeah," she whispered. "I forgot to tell you. The ants returned to their queen and made a new army." And with that she disappeared further down into the darkness of the hole.

Leaf wondered if he should skedaddle back, away from the advancing column of ants, or continue lying where he was. He wasn't sure what to do, but then remembered the Triple A's. *Oh, yeah, okay, where am I in the list? Where there's one – more to come....no; Stop your play – run away...no, too late; If trapped lay down flat...that's me now. What should I do?*

He raised his head to see if he could spot where the column was moving but he was too low in the furrow to see anything but dirt. He wanted desperately to remember the rest of the list.

Do best – warn rest. That's it, he thought, and then berated himself for rugging out so quickly. He felt helpless lying on the ground, partly because he didn't know where the enemy was marching.

What if they turned and went another way? he thought. *I could lay here for hours for nothing.* And then he had a chilling thought. *What if they turned and are heading for the tree?* That thought did it and he decided to stand up and skedaddle away. He was about to do it when he heard a voice.

"Clear!" the voice called and then three other voices responded the same.

"Clear!"

"Clear!"

"Clear!"

Leaf froze. Must be the ant scouts, he thought, and sure enough they were but a foot away and moving quickly, checking every nook and cranny of the furrow.

"Tell the sergeant, no rabbits," the lead ant said. "Looks like groundhogs, check?"

"Check!" a scout replied. "No rabbits – looks like groundhogs."

"Check," the lead ant confirmed and stepped onto Leaf's leg.

Leaf froze in horror, holding his breath and trying to will his thumping heart to beat quietly.

CHAPTER EIGHT

WORMS TO THE WEST

Twig and Nut were sitting on the dock where the *Flying Vine* was moored, watching the crewmen work in a long line passing cargo to each other from the hold of the ship to the docks. Leaf's father was directing the activity from the deck, and Thicket Figthorn stood on the dock talking to Rake's father, Wedge Raven, and Stump's father, Knot Nettletick. The three were trying to speak quietly, but they weren't being very successful. Twig could tell that Wedge was very upset about something, so he grabbed Nut and moved a little closer to the three men so he could hear them better.

"It's time, I say," Wedge said.

"It's time when I say it's time," said Thicket.

"It's only ten o'clock," said Knot, which made the other two look at him as if he was crazy.

"Haven't you been listening to us?" asked Wedge. "Sometimes you are so dense you…"

"Never mind that, Wedge," said Thicket. "Right now is not the time. Listen, this afternoon is the Tree Council meeting. Eric the 'Dead' Leaf is bound to say something about the trees. He didn't sneak off at the Coastal settlement for nothing. No matter what he says, there isn't anyone who's going to believe him. The council members are tired of his ranting, and I've made sure to drill it into each one of their heads till they are sick of talking about it. Oakreach will pull out the maps again and then we'll pounce!"

"We're gonna hit him?" asked Knot. Wedge moaned and rolled his eyes.

"No, but Red Leaf will feel like he's been hit in the gut by a tail-spinning one-winged bumblebee," said Thicket. "When he left us so long at the bay, the rest of the crew was almost ready to leave without him. And you should have seen them when we sailed for so long and didn't find anything but treeless rocky islands. They've completely lost faith in his judgment. Those crew members are on the council, and they give me enough votes to get him removed from leadership. All I have to do is stand up and ask for a vote. After he's removed there will be a call for a new leader and that's where you come in."

"You want me to be the new leader?" said Knot loudly.

"Shhh," Thicket hissed and slapped Knot on the back of his head.

"No, Nettletick. Wedge will nominate me and you'll second the nomination. After that, I'll be in charge. Think of it. Finally, this tree will have someone with vision and strength. We'll build warships and train more soldiers. We'll find the ant colonies and wipe out each one of them once and for all. We'll hunt down the caterpillars and the termites; we'll tame the spiders and the beetles; we'll demand acorn payments from the squirrels, and honey from the bees. When I'm in charge, we'll dominate the forest! No one will stand in my way!"

"*Our* way," corrected Wedge.

"Oh, yes," Thicket admitted reluctantly. "No one will stand in our way!"

Twig was beside himself as he watched the three men congratulate each other for their plan as they walked back toward the ship. He didn't know what to do, but he knew he had to find Leaf. Somehow, Leaf's father had to be warned. Nut took off his helmet and scratched his head.

"Was he saying what I think he was saying, Twig?"

"Yeah, Nut," Twig answered. "Like son, like father."

The two friends jumped up, caught air, and headed for Leaf's house.

Garland stood outside the doorway of her home and smelled the spring air. She had been cooped up inside most of the morning doing chores and was finally free to enjoy the day.

Taking in a deep breath, she turned to spy a little yellow vine-flower growing beside the door.

"You need water, don't you?" she said to the flower and was about to go back inside to get some water when she heard voices through the branches.

"If he's not at home, where could he be?" Twig said.

"I don't know," Nut answered. "Maybe he was going down to the dock when we were coming up. We have to find him, Twig!"

Garland could tell from Nut's voice that he was upset. The boys were moving quickly skyward so she promised the vine-flower she would return, caught air, and flew up after them.

Leaf lay on the ground as still as a frozen stick in December. Ants, hundreds of them it seemed, had come and gone, with most of them stepping right on top of him. Twice they had tickled his neck with their feet and once an antenna had poked him in the nose. He didn't have to will himself not to giggle from the tickle, but he did have to stifle a sneeze.

The ant scouts had, of course, searched the rabbit hole, but they reported the groundhog long gone. Leaf heard them do a lot of reporting. The scouts reported in to the sergeant and the sergeant reported in to the lieutenant. The lieutenant reported in to the captain and the captain reported in to the major. The major reported in to the colonel and the colonel had reported in to the general. Leaf heard each one and thought that, even though the ants were very efficient, they didn't seem very flexible in their ability to do anything without reporting.

At one point he had heard them talk about a grasshopper that had been discovered nearby, but by the time all the reports had gone up the chain of command, the grasshopper had hopped away. Then, in the middle of their reporting that the grasshopper had hopped away, he hopped back into sight again, creating such confusion that the ants didn't know what to do.

Leaf would have laughed about it, except for the last hour he had been constantly surrounded by marching ants and was in no laughing mood. His body was stiff from lying in the same position, and his nerves were on edge from the threat of being discovered. He had to find a way out of his predicament, and the grasshopper incident had given him an idea. He picked the right moment when there were gaps in the lines of the ant columns, and as best he could, mimicked a scout.

"Check!" Leaf called out. "Fresh worms running west! Check!"

All of a sudden ant voices called out from every direction, and Leaf could hear their little feet flying.

"Check! Worms to the west! Worms to the west! Check!"

"Check!"

"Check!"

As he had hoped, all of the ants around him headed west away from him and away from the tree. He looked around carefully, saw that the coast was clear, and was about to make his way back home to the east, when a commanding voice called out, "Cancel that order and return to the trail!"

Leaf's heart sank as he heard the responses of the other ants as they turned back. The voice called out again and Leaf lifted his head a little and peeked with one eye to see who was speaking. It was the ant general and he was only a few feet away.

"Get those men back in line," he called out. "No one breaks rank from now on until I give the order. Do you understand me?"

There was a chorus of "Yes, sirs," and shouts for everyone to get back into column formation. Leaf studied the general and noticed he walked with a limp, had a broken antennae, and a scar on his cheek. Leaf wondered if he had ever met Anson the Antthumper, and then figured the general couldn't be old enough to have done battle with the famous hero of days gone by. No, he was probably trampled by his own men when they were chasing after a centipede.

Leaf chuckled to himself, but a shadow suddenly passed overhead and ruined the moment. All of the ants cringed in terror except the general. He stood at attention as a red breasted robin landed nearby and cautiously approached. Leaf thought it strange that a robin would come so near the aggressive ants. Robins had always been kind creatures, and at the least, cordial with members of the Colony.

"Well?" the general asked the robin. "Tell me what I want to know or you know what happens."

"Where are my young?" the robin asked anxiously.

"Safe in their shells, I assure you," the general responded. "I promised you that no ant would harm them."

"I want to see them!" the robin demanded.

"You're in no position to order me to do anything," the general yelled back.

"I could eat you right now!" the robin said and took a step closer. The general didn't flinch.

"And my men will have eggs for breakfast."

The robin stopped in her tracks and lowered her head. She seemed to be wrestling with what to do. Her head quivered back and forth and she swallowed hard. She opened her mouth, closed it, and then opened it again.

"They are to the east," the robin said faintly, and Leaf's heart sank.

"What was that?" the general said pretending not to hear. "I didn't quite catch that."

The robin took a deep breath. "They are not far to the east, in a large oak past the blackberry patch and before the creek."

CHAPTER NINE
ONION GRASS SOUFFLÉ

About ten yards away in a pine tree, Twig, Nut and Garland sat high enough on a branch to see the robin, but they weren't high enough to see Leaf or the general who were down in the rabbit furrow. They had spotted the ants heading off to the west to find the worms and also watched them return.

"Do you think the robin is talking to Leaf?" Nut asked.

"I don't know," said Twig. "The groundhog said he was close by in Rabbit's Run, but there are a lot of ants there."

"Why is the robin standing in the middle of the column?" Garland asked. "She must be surrounded by ants and she's not moving!"

The three had circled the tree calling for Leaf before heading into open air. They had landed close to the blackberry patch and were about to return home when they heard the groundhog pop up from a tunnel, out of breath.

"Ants, ants, ants," they heard her grumble. "The talking leaf wasn't thinking. I told him to keep moving!" She had started for another hole when the three intercepted her and asked her what she meant. That's when they found out what had happened and figured Leaf had rugged out.

Twig wanted to skedaddle right on over to Rabbit's Run, but Garland suggested taking a high route so they could spy out the situation. It wouldn't do them any good to run right into the ant column.

"Maybe the robin is protecting Leaf," Garland said.

"Maybe Leaf is protecting the robin," Twig said.

"Maybe Leaf isn't even there," Nut said. Twig and Garland looked at Nut and no one said a word. In their hearts they all wished Nut was right.

Down below, the general ordered preparations for the column to head east. He also called for runners to report back to the queen.

"Tell her we found them and that revenge for past defeats will soon be mine—er, I mean hers! And also tell her to bring up the other two columns. I want three brigades of leaf-cutters, two brigades of termites, and cavalry! Get me lots of cavalry!"

At that, Leaf figured that since the ants now knew where the Colony was located it didn't matter if he broke rule number five, "Don't lead them here – get free and clear."

I have to get home and do my best to warn the rest, he thought, but the general called out again.

"Bring the robin her eggs!" At that, some thirty wolf-spiders came hustling down the trail carrying two little blue eggs on their shoulders. The robin started for her eggs, but the general raised his hand to stop her.

"Not so fast, birdie," the general hissed. "I promised you that no ant would harm your eggs, but my allies the wolf-spiders have worked very hard to not get some kind of reward. One of your eggs ought to do."

"No!" the robin yelled.

"Have at it, boys!" the general said to the wolf-spiders, but before they could lower the eggs from their shoulders, Leaf rose up, skedaddled over, grabbed the two eggs and caught air. It wasn't easy, especially since a spider and an ant hung on to his feet, but robins' eggs were light, and Leaf had practiced catching air while holding acorns and even rocks.

The spider and the ant were a dangerous nuisance, though. The ant was climbing up Leaf's left leg and the spider kept trying to bite his right foot. Leaf kicked with his leg and flicked his foot in an effort to get free from their grasps, but all he managed to do was twirl into a spin and almost lose hold of an egg. He had to brace the slipping egg with his chin, which put him into a tuck and made him lose air even faster. He was heading for the ground and was going to slam smack dab into a platoon of angry ants when Garland caught him and helped him to rise. The spider on Leaf's foot opened its mouth to take a bite out of Garland, but an out-of-control Nut rammed it with his acorn-helmeted head and sent it hurtling off into the bushes. Twig flew over and grabbed the ant and flung him back toward the general.

"Take that!" Twig yelled, and even though the ant missed, it did make the general flinch and fall backward on his crippled leg, which was a good thing for him because the robin went to take a quick bite of his head. Ants closed in all around her so she didn't chance another try –instead, she flew off to catch up to Leaf.

Garland grabbed one of the eggs from Leaf and directed him to the perch above where she and Twig and Nut had sat watching. The robin was on her way up, too, when they all heard a scream and turned to look behind them. Nut was floating down helplessly toward the ground. His helmet, squashed from the impact with the spider, was over his face and covering his eyes. He was frantically trying to catch air but couldn't, and the ants were patiently waiting below.

Back home, Leaf's mom was preparing Eric's favorite lunch of nettle nuts and daisy gravy with onion grass on the side. It was a ritual they'd had since the first time he returned from a long expedition. She would ask him at breakfast what he wanted for lunch and he would say "Nuts and gravy, please." She would ask, "Are you sure?" and he would reply, "Maybe onion grass soufflé instead." She would shake her head and moan, "You are the only one in this family who likes onion grass soufflé. What about the rest of us?" He would lean back in his chair and rub his chin as if he had a tough decision to make. "Okay," he would finally say. "Nuts and gravy it is." She would hug him and kiss his head, and then he would ask in a pleading five-year-old tone, "Could I have a little onion grass on the side?" It was an endearing little ritual and they would laugh like kids each time.

This morning, though, she felt uneasy as she prepared to cook. She worried about the upcoming meeting in the afternoon, especially since Eric had told her what he had found. Even if all the trees of the forest were to disappear, most of the Colony wouldn't believe Eric. The proof would have to come from someone else—someone they believed in. The thought made her sad for him, and for the future of the Colony.

Who would they elect if Eric was voted out? The answer she came up with was a bitter bug to swallow.

After lunch, she put on her finest floral dress and sat in the living room brushing her hair with the clam-comb Eric had made for her during one of his voyages. He had found the clam on a small island and had cut and shaped it during the long months out at sea. It had a beautiful iridescent pink and silver color and was smoothly grooved so her long hair wouldn't tangle. She saw Eric come out of the bedroom and her jaw dropped. She had expected him to be wearing his formal captain's outfit, but instead he was wearing a normal dress tunic.

"Why are you wearing that?" she asked. "What about your uniform?"

"I'm not going to wear it, because today, no matter whether they believe me or not, I'm resigning my commission and stepping down from leadership of the Colony."

If her jaw could have fallen further, it would have hit the floor.

CHAPTER TEN
THE HUNT

Shady, Rake, and Stump had also been busy during the beautiful Wednesday morning. Unfortunately, they had no idea what "beautiful" meant.

They had started off walking around in a bored daze until a foraging squirrel happened to catch their eye. With slingshots in hand, they took off after it, following it from tree to tree and firing acorns and pebbles at the poor creature for several hours. They were relentless in their pursuit, reaching to the heights and depths of the trees constantly trying to outflank the squirrel in order to get off their shots. Twice they hit him and, when he wailed in agony, it sent shivers of joy down their twisted leafy veins.

At last, they cornered him at the end of a branch, and in his haste the squirrel misjudged the distance of his leap to another tree and fell twenty levels below into a thicket of giant burley-thorns. The three miscreants quickly lost air to ground level and skedaddled to the thicket. The squirrel lay dazed in a tangled mass of vines and thorns, his chest heaving for air and his heart beating wildly.

"We have him cornered now," Rake said, and went to the left side firing shots, but the thorns caused the missiles to deflect. Shady fired with the same result.

"Work in a little closer, Stump," Shady said, moving to the right. "Get some of those vines out of the way so we can shoot." But Stump was exhausted and stood there with his hands on his knees trying to catch his breath.

"Okay," Stump gasped. "Give me a second."

"No! Do it now!" Shady ordered. Stump stood upright, took in some more air and trudged forward. He took several cautious steps, moved a few thorny vines out of the way, and slowly stepped toward the squirrel. He wasn't moving fast enough for Shady.

"Get in there!" Shady yelled and fired a shot, hitting Stump in the backside.

"Ow!" The big fellow yelled and stumbled headlong into the thicket, cutting his face, hands, arms and legs on the jagged giant prickles. He hung suspended in air by the vines a few feet from the squirrel.

"Good job," Rake said sarcastically. "Now he's completely blocking our shot."

"No, he's not," said Shady with wicked glee, and fired another one into Stump's backside, causing the big boy to howl. "I have a perfect line of sight."

Rake fired too, and then they both let off a barrage until they were out of ammunition and Stump was out of tears. It wasn't Stump's day. As he lay moaning in the vines the squirrel gingerly worked free from the thorns, carefully hopped over and bit him on the nose. He couldn't tell what hurt worse, the thorns, the slingshot pellets, or the squirrel bite.

With nothing to shoot with, Shady and Rake could only watch as the squirrel made its way out of the thicket and up into the trees. As they yanked on Stump's feet to pull him out of the thicket, they were unaware of the threat behind them. An entire company of mounted ant scouts arrived on the backs of fanged wolf-spiders. With the thicket to their backs and over their heads, the boys were surrounded with nowhere to go.

Shady froze. For the first time in his life he was faced with a situation that a conniving nasty attitude couldn't fix. Rake clung to him like a scared spider hanging on to his web in a thunderstorm. Stump broke the silence.

"Those are ants," he said matter-of-factly. "I didn't know they could ride spiders."

Before Shady could respond, the ant captain in charge had ordered a scout to report back to the general, directed his troops to tighten the ring around the three boys, and dismounted. He approached Shady.

"Lay down your weapons and surrender," the captain demanded. "Or we'll shred you where you stand." The ants kicked their heels into the wolf-spiders, whose huge fangs dripped with saliva as they snarled grotesquely.

Shady had forgotten he was even holding his slingshot. In an instant, he thought he might have a way out. He brought it up, pulled back the sling, and aimed it at the captain.

"You might shred us but I'm gonna get you first," he threatened.

The captain took a step back. Shady smiled, but not for long.

"You're out of ammo, remember, Shady?" Stump said. "I know you are cause you would'a kept shoot'n me, and I…."

"Shut up, Stump!" Shady growled but it was too late. It was the captain's turn to smile as he issued his order.

"Take them!"

As the ants prodded the wolf-spiders toward their prey, Shady pulled away from Rake's grasp and raised his sling like a club. He wasn't going down without a fight.

Leaf watched helplessly as Nut floated closer and closer to the waiting ants. Even though they were on a branch, Garland still held onto him and he and Twig were still holding the robin's eggs.

"Nut!" Garland cried out. "We have to save Nut!"

The three looked to the robin who was about to land on the branch next to them. All she wanted to do was make sure her babies were safe and get them as far away from the ants as possible, but Garland's cry had sent a shiver down her wings. She pushed away from the branch with her talons and shot down to Nut in a flash. As Nut finally managed to get his crushed helmet off of his head, he was face-to-face with a group of ants reaching up to grab him. The robin snatched him up just in time with her beak and rushed him back to the branch.

"Th…th…thank you!" Nut stammered, having never taken a ride in a bird's beak before.

"Yes, thank you," Garland added.

"You're welcome," the robin said and looked to Leaf. "Thank you for saving my babies. You could have stayed hidden and not put yourself in any danger but you didn't—especially since I gave away the location of your tree. I'm so sorry, and I'm so grateful for what you did."

"You are welcome, ma'am," Leaf said.

Leaf looked below and saw the scope of the ant forces. It was a huge column, and with the menace of two more like it, along with leaf-cutters, termites and wolf-spiders, he realized he had to act quickly. He turned to the robin.

"Let's get you and the eggs to safety and then we have to go warn the Colony."

"I prepared a place already in a tree not far from yours," she said, "but far enough away from it to be safe." She thought about what she had said and was ashamed. "I'm so sorry, I can't explain…"

"We understand," Garland interrupted. "You didn't really have much of a choice."

"We need to go," Twig whispered to Leaf.

"Okay, lead the way, ma'am," Leaf said to the Robin. "We'll carry the babies."

And with that they headed east, Leaf and Twig carrying the eggs, Garland helping Nut, and the robin flying from branch to branch in front of them. Soon they were well ahead of the ants and breathed a little easier, seeing the extent of the distance the ants would have to cover before reaching the tree.

CHAPTER ELEVEN
YOUR MAJESTY

"They're looking at you in your civvies," Leaf's mom said to Eric as they walked arm-in-arm down the center thoroughfare branch toward the Tree Council chambers. It seemed that everyone who saw them stopped to stare and point out the fact that Eric wasn't wearing his formals.

"No, darling, they are looking at you in your beautiful dress," Eric replied. "You are one stunning civilian's girl."

"I'm a woman, Mister Red Leaf!"

"I like the sound of that," Eric mused.

"The woman part or the mister?" she asked.

"Both."

They giggled and ignored the gawking, behaving as if it were only the two of them on the branch. As they rounded the corner of the block in front of the council chambers, they ran into Principal Oakreach hurrying down another lane.

"Afternoon, Eric," the principal said, while trying to hide the cylindrical tubes he carried behind his back. "And how are you, Mrs. Red Leaf?"

"I'm fine, Principal Oakreach," she said, spying the tubes. "My, but

Leaf sure did appreciate your kindness in showing him your maps yesterday at school."

The principal's eyes bugged out and he coughed. "Yes, yes," he stammered. "My pleasure. My pleasure." And off he went, scurrying into the council chambers.

"I can't believe you sometimes," Eric whispered.

"At least he didn't seem to notice what you were wearing."

But everyone else did. Only a moment before, the place had been stirring with conversations in every corner, but when they entered, it went as silent as a beehive in January.

Eric led her to her seat and then took the podium. The rest of the council quickly found their seats, except for Thicket Figthorn, Wedge Raven, and Knot Nettletick. The three conspirators slowly ambled to their seats, in obvious disdain of their leader. Figthorn turned and stared hard at the other members of the council as he sat down. Leaf's mom felt a little queasy as Eric cleared his throat and began to speak.

Leaf gently placed the fragile egg into the nest that had already been readied by the robin. Twig did the same with the one he carried. Garland tenderly patted the tiny orbs.

"There, there, you darlings," she said. "You're all safe and sound now."

"Thank you all," said the robin. "I wish there was something that I could do for you." She thought a second and then added. "Do you know where you will go?"

"I'm not sure, but my father is the leader of our Colony and he wants us to leave the forest as soon as possible," Leaf answered. "He's been searching for the right place, but I don't think he has found it yet." Twig, Nut and Garland gave Leaf a surprised look.

"And when were you going to tell us that?" Garland asked pointedly.

"Is this about the trees disappearing?" Twig added sarcastically.

"Yes, the Coastals are…"

"Oh, come on, Leaf," Garland said with annoyance. "Focus on the problem at hand. The ants are the menace. The Coastals don't have anything to do with…"

"They are getting closer," the robin interrupted.

Twig, Nut and Garland quickly looked down to the ground for the ants.

"Where?" Nut asked. "I don't see them."

"Not the ants," the robin said, "the Coastals, as you call them. We call them, 'Chaaawp' for the sound they make when they cut down trees. They have five villages surrounding us and are building more and more roads every day. They are chaaawping down trees by the hundreds."

Twig, Nut, and Garland fell silent and turned to Leaf. Leaf explained what his father had mapped and about the Coastals finding a place, but not knowing what to do with it.

"Dad will probably find a safe spot for now and then go on another voyage to find the Coastal's place. At least that's what I would do."

Garland looked at Leaf long and hard, and took him by the hand.

"I'm sorry for not believing you," she said softly.

"Yeah, me, too," added Twig.

Nut was silent, so they all looked his way.

"What?" Nut shrugged innocently. "I don't even know what you guys are talking about."

"We need to get you another helmet," Leaf said.

The three said good-bye to the robin and headed off toward the tree. It was getting late in the afternoon and the sun was heading away from them. They caught air, rose several levels and maneuvered through a thickly bunched grove of beech, elm and oak trees. Leaf and Twig sped ahead while Garland again fell back to help Nut, who was having a difficult time zooming through the breaks of a large elm.

"You can do it, Nut," Garland encouraged. "Keep your speed and turn sideways."

"Okay," Nut said, but then rammed into the side of a large branch. He fell backward, flipped, and spiraled downward toward the lower levels faster than a frozen pine cone.

"Leaf! Twig! Stop!" Garland yelled, but the boys were too far ahead to hear. Nut was falling so rapidly Garland gave up yelling and headed downward, tucking and zooming as fast as she could. When she reached the ground she expected to find Nut crumbled up in the roots, but instead she found him dazed but unhurt sitting on what looked like a fur rug.

"It broke my fall," Nut said with a chuckle. "It's pretty soft but prickly and also kind of squishy."

Garland looked closely at what lay beneath Nut and gasped, putting her hand to her mouth. Nut saw her expression—a mixture of wonder, disgust and fear.

"What is it?" Nut asked. "What's the matter?"

"Get up, and I'll know for sure."

When Nut went to stand up he put his hand down as a brace and it stuck in some sticky goo.

"Ewww!" Nut moaned. "What is this?" He jumped up quickly, flicking his hand to get rid of the sticky substance.

"Wolf-spider!" Garland shouted. "I knew it!"

Nut looked and sure enough, he had been sitting on a giant squished spider. Nut began wiping his hand on anything he could find; grass, leaves, twigs, bark and dirt.

"I have wolf-spider guts all over my hand. Yuck!"

Garland spied some movement in the grass behind Nut and ske-daddled over quickly to find a half-conscious ant lying on his back with his legs flailing.

"And what have we here?" she asked.

The ant looked at Garland and smiled. His head swooned with triple vision and, in his concussed condition, he thought she was his queen.

"Check, check," he moaned. "Captured three enemy leaves due east. Check, check, Your Majesty." He paused for a moment and then added. "Excuse me, ma'am, but I am going to throw up." He did and passed out.

"I'm going to be sick, too," Nut added.

"Not now, you're not!" Garland ordered. "Let's move!"

She grabbed Nut, pointed him to the east and skedaddled.

CHAPTER TWELVE

SWEET NECTAR

Leaf and Twig raced like they always did and soon forgot about their slower companions. They were in their element of flying through the trees and their purpose was urgent. They had to get back to the tree and warn the Colony. Up and down they flew, catching air and descending to weave their way through everything they encountered.

"Come on, Twig, move!"

"I'm moving as fast as you!"

And so he was. Twig had kept pace with Leaf the whole way, but they arrived at a V at the same time and got themselves crammed together. They hurt themselves good but had to laugh at their predicament, stuck together like wheat bugs trying to eat the same piece of grain. They both wiggled and giggled and finally gave up trying to force their way apart, and that's when they plopped out unexpectedly and fell to the branch below with a thud.

"Ow!" they both said and then laughed some more. They lay there for a few seconds, and then looked back the way they had come.

"I wonder what happened to those two slow-boats," Leaf asked.

"I bet they didn't stick together inside a V," Twig answered.

"They probably didn't even make it through a....." Leaf stopped abruptly. "Did you hear that?"

"Hear what?"

"I thought I heard a..." As he spoke, someone down on ground level let out a horrific scream of pain. They jumped up, scanned the forest floor and saw movement in the roots of the great tree.

"Come on," Leaf said, and he and Twig headed downward.

"Let go of me!" Shady screamed as a big army ant crammed a moss-gag back into his mouth. "I'm gonna cut your antennae off of your...hmmmmhmmmm," was all Shady could say as the gag was stuck back in place. A moment before, an ant had bit him on his hand for removing the gag, and that was the scream Leaf and Twig had heard.

Shady had his hands tied behind his back, as did Rake and Stump who were behind him. The three were being marched in a line joined together by a vine lassoed around their necks, and pulled by a great big ant riding atop a wolf-spider. Most of the patrol was in front of the captives, but only five ants and their spiders guarded the rear.

"They have those boys for sure," Leaf whispered to Twig from their perch on the lowest branch level.

"They can keep Rake," Twig whispered back.

"I have a better idea," Leaf said. "Let's get some swords and chop off some heads!"

"Yeah," Twig agreed, secretly hoping Leaf meant Rake's head as well.

The two headed for the far side of the tree and quickly dropped to the floor to forage for the right type of sticks. They found two perfect short pointy ones for swords and a couple long enough for spears. Leaf signaled Twig to skedaddle after him to the side of the tree trunk to lay an ambush. As the lead ants went by, Leaf planned to attack the rear guard and free

Shady, Rake, and Stump so they could all catch air to safety. At least, that was the plan.

As the captain and the lead ants went by, Leaf braced himself to spring. He nodded to Twig.

"Now," Leaf said softly.

At the moment they rose up, the ant captain halted his troop. Someone was singing on the trail ahead. Leaf heard the voice too and stopped. She sang a sad lyric with a happy lilt.

Sweet nectar
Sweet nectar
My love's gone away
He's lost on the ocean
Or tossed on the bay
His ship won't be back
For many a day
Sweet nectar
Sweet nectar
My love's gone away

Garland held a freshly picked bouquet of flowers, and was spinning and dancing on top of a small log of fallen timber. Before Leaf could say or do anything, the ant captain had ordered three riders forward. The wolf-spiders snarled and sped toward their prey. The ant riders smiled with delight, but Garland didn't seem to notice.

Leaf screamed, "No!"

The ants spurred their spider's forward and leapt at Garland, who turned to them with a smile.

"Now!" Garland yelled.

Below her and hidden in the brush on either side, two strong young caterpillars pulled back on their net of freshly spun cocoon thread, raising it in the air. The spiders and their riders slammed into it and, though it gave with their force as if to carry them within inches of Garland's face, the thread held them tightly.

The ant captain sent three more riders, but as they approached, Garland reached down and picked up a bow and several arrows she had hastily made for the occasion. Nut hopped up beside her on the log with his own bow. Garland shot two of the spiders, stopping them in their tracks, which hurled their ant riders into the net.

Nut fired at the third, but missed completely. His arrow went over its head and straight at the ant captain, who ducked. It landed with a thunk in the chest of the big ant that led Shady, Rake, and Stump.

The ant Nut had aimed at laughed and spurred his spider forward, running under the net and up the log. He was inches from Nut when Garland ran over and knocked the ant off of the spider with her bow and, without missing a beat, jumped on top of the wolf-spider.

Before the spider could throw her off, Nut grabbed an arrow, pulled back the bow string and aimed. Garland didn't know which was worse— being on top of a crazed wolf-spider or having Nut point a bow and arrow in her direction. She closed her eyes. So did Nut.

Luckily, the ant that had been knocked off the spider by Garland crawled up to Nut and grabbed his foot. It made Nut jerk his arms and, when the arrow was loosed, it hit the spider right in the head and dropped him in his tracks. Garland hopped off the dead spider and grabbed the ant from Nut's foot and flung him into the caterpillar's netting.

Meanwhile, Leaf and Twig attacked the five riders in the back. Leaf speared an ant's leg and pinned it to his spider's side. The two yelped in pain and ran off, the spider bucking like a bull and the ant flailing helplessly on board.

Twig threw his spear and missed an ant's head by inches, but made the ant fall off his spider. The spider turned and lunged at Twig, but Leaf ran up and rammed his sword into its throat. The ant ran away into the woods.

Dismayed, the ants rode off in every direction. The captain called out to them to halt and stand their ground, but it was too late. With Garland and Nut taking aim with their bows, and Leaf and Twig approaching from behind, the captain kicked his heels into his spider and headed off to the west. The battle was over in less than a minute.

Shady, Rake, and Stump wiggled on the ground, trying to free themselves from their ropes. Garland and Nut joined Leaf and Twig beside them and removed their gags.

"Get these vines off of us," Shady demanded.

"How about a thank you?" Garland suggested.

"Thank you," said Stump.

"Yeah, thanks," Rake said and turned to Twig. "Thanks for missing me with that spear you hurled. You throw like a girl."

"Watch it, buddy," Garland said. It was then she saw the ant bite on Shady's hand. She bent down, took his hand and spit on the wound.

"Thank you!" Shady exclaimed with a big grin, and then glanced at Leaf, who was watching with a look of disgust. "Thank you very much."

"Great. This is simply great," Leaf complained.

Garland turned her head to look back at Leaf. "Were you going to do it?" she replied.

"He could have done it himself," Leaf whined.

"His hands are tied behind his back," Garland said, shaking her head with disappointment. "Really, Leaf, you….oh, never mind."

Leaf walked away, mumbling to himself, to survey the dead ants and spiders. Twig stood in front of a tied-up Rake and aimed his sword at his head.

"What do you want?" Rake muttered, and then his eyes opened wide as Twig brought the sword down quickly. Rake shut his eyes in fright, but all Twig did was cut the ropes.

"Fly away, little Raven, fly away," Twig sang.

"Very funny," Rake said sarcastically.

"All right!" Leaf exclaimed. "It's going to be dark soon. We need to get back to the tree now!"

"You scared of the dark?" Shady teased.

Leaf caught air and hovered.

"I'll tell you what I'm scared of on the way home." And with that, he was off.

CHAPTER THIRTEEN
SECONDS AND THIRDS

With the sun setting quickly, Eric the Red Leaf stared at the floor of the great hall as Thicket Figthorn addressed the assembly. After Eric had opened the meeting, Figthorn immediately called for "Open Discussions" and took over the dais. He had been speaking for twenty minutes about all the things Eric had done wrong since taking office.

"…not to mention the reduction in our armed forces," Thicket said.

A chorus of "Ayes!" affirmed his words from all around the hall.

"And that brings us to his latest failure to lead the expedition—an expedition that none of us wanted to take in the first place. He has reduced our armed forces budget in order to embark on a series of senseless excursions to find a new place to live. Now, I don't know about you, but I don't see anything wrong with where we are living now."

A resounding "Aye!" filled the place. Leaf's mom turned to Eric. He raised his head, smiled and winked at her. She was too worried to return the smile or the wink.

"And while on this self-aggrandizing expedition," Thicket continued, "he abandoned the ship to disappear into the forest for several days. When he finally returned, without an explanation, he led us out to sea to some horribly barren treeless islands. And, when we were about starved to death, he suddenly changed course to lead us home so we could make it back in time for his son's boat race."

The place filled with "Boos!"

"If that's not the most irresponsibly selfish example of failed leadership this Colony has ever known, then I don't know what is." Thicket pounded his fist on the dais, and angry voices reverberated throughout the hall.

"A vote!" someone shouted and then another.

"A vote!"

"A vote!"

"A vote!" They all called out.

Thicket nodded at Wedge Raven. "I demand the removal of Eric the Red Leaf from leadership!" Wedge exclaimed. Knot Nettletick looked to Thicket as if to say, "Now?" Thicket nodded.

"Um, I, ah, I second this, I think, or is it I agree?" Knot mumbled.

"All in favor?" Thicket said.

"Aye!" was the seemingly unanimous response.

Thicket smiled and nodded to Wedge again.

"I nominate Thicket Figthorn to lead the Colony!" Wedge yelled.

Eric stood up and announced, "I second the nomination!"

Knot Nettletick squirmed in his seat and shouted, "I third!"

The place went quiet except for a few moans and some chuckles. All eyes were on Eric.

"If you don't want me to lead you anymore," Eric said, "and if you think Thicket Figthorn can do a better job, then I will stand by the majority rule of the council and support the Colony and its leadership one hundred percent—as always. Let there be a vote!"

The assembly remained silent. Even Figthorn was speechless, but a smile gradually spread across his face.

"Oh, and by the way," Eric said. "You may have noticed I did not dress in my uniform. I had already decided that no matter what happened tonight, I was resigning."

Figthorn's smile broadened.

"And it doesn't even matter," Eric added, "if you don't want to see the new map showing the new Coastal settlements and their new roads."

Thicket Figthorn lost his smile and squirmed in his seat. He knew he couldn't rush things to a vote when there was the possibility of a threat to the Colony. The council would see it as a breach of priority. He would have to let things play out, and he would have to seem concerned. He cleared his throat.

"Yes, by all means, I think we should take a look at this new map," Figthorn admitted. "Principal Oakreach, would you please examine it, and of course, compare it to the official maps in your possession."

Principal Oakreach gathered his maps and rose from his chair. He was about to walk toward Eric, when the council chamber doors burst open wide. Seven wide-eyed children rushed breathlessly inside. Leaf ran to his dad.

"Dad? Dad! Ants!" Leaf exclaimed. "The ants are coming!"

The commotion in the chamber wasn't going to settle down quickly, despite the efforts of Thicket Figthorn. Small groups of men impulsively gathered to prepare defensive measures.

Yet Figthorn still wanted a vote and he shouted over the commotion to get everyone to retake their seats. No one paid him much attention. As Leaf was telling his father and mother about the day's events, Eric watched the council members and decided it was time to change things if he could. Defending a place that was going to eventually be lost anyway didn't make any sense. Why lose lives to an enemy if there is no reason to fight the battle? Eric rose and took the dais.

"A vote!" Eric commanded. "A vote was called for tonight!"

"I propose we table the vote!" said a member.

"I second!" said another. "All in favor...."

"No!" screamed Eric. "That simply won't do! Now listen to me!"

The council members finally stopped talking and some returned to their seats, while most stood and turned to face the dais where they were.

"You don't have to be happy with me," he confided, his tone seemingly indifferent. "I'm not here to win your favor. All I want is your ear for one short moment." Eric paused and surveyed the room.

"Gentlemen, I have seen the Coastal's villages," he said. As expected, the muttering began. He spoke above the din. "That's right, villages. I have seen five, as a matter of fact, and each one is connected by roads, with more roads leading to I don't know where—probably more villages. They have completely surrounded the forest, and have already made a tremendous impact on the tree population. It won't be long before they arrive here—possibly before my children's children are born. That may seem like a lifetime to some, but if we fight this battle tomorrow, then some of us won't have a lifetime at all. There is no sense fighting if we have to leave…"

"What are you saying, Red Leaf?" interrupted Thicket Figthorn. "You want us to run away from the tree? You want us to abandon the Colony? You want everyone to leave now, because in a couple of generations we'll have to leave anyway? Are you kidding? We have been here forever! You wanted to resign earlier tonight and now we know the real reason behind it. You are a coward and a traitor to everything we believe in. You sully the names of Anson the Antthumper, Bastion the Brownstick, and all the fine leaves here ready to defend our land."

The place went nuts. Before Leaf knew what had happened, a vote was taken and Thicket Figthorn was voted the new leader. Some had called for Eric to be imprisoned for treason, but others said the threat of war came first and that everyone was needed to defend the Colony. They couldn't spare even one guard to watch him, so why bother. Eric became a non-entity, and Leaf felt sick to his stomach. His whole world was collapsing.

CHAPTER FOURTEEN
THREE THROUGH ELEVEN

The strategy to defend the Colony was simple. The tree was already surrounded by the creek, but once they heard that the ants were coming, trenches were quickly dug to expand the natural flow of the creek. With the trenches, the creek not only encircled the tree, but moved the water outwardly as well, like a child's drawing of the sun's rays. The channels would serve to funnel an ant attack to specific places where the Colony's defense was strongest.

To bolster defenses, hundreds of caterpillars and spiders—who had long been the leaves' allies—worked tirelessly to form their sticky netting into an impenetrable wall that completely surrounded the tree and the funnels. Camouflaged archer stations were hung from vines on the overhanging branches to cover each funnel approach. Above them javelin throwers, acorn droppers, and rock slingers were positioned. The tree was also ringed with catapult launchers that could hurl twenty large thorn-arrows at a time.

Knowing that some of the ants would want to enter the waterways to avoid the walls, the defenders placed hundreds of deliciously irresistible, floating blueberries spiked with wasp venom. Vines crisscrossed the waterways to keep the blueberries from floating out and into the creek.

Catapults were also readied to sling poisoned berries into the approaching army to cause a disruption as the ants broke ranks to eat them—and eventually die.

Lastly, the entire trunk of the tree was coated in honey and tree sap. If the ants got that far, they wouldn't be able to move through that sticky coating. The defenders worked tirelessly during the night to make sure all of the defenses were in place.

Twig and Nut dug trenches, sharpened arrows, toted acorns and rocks, and filled waterways with blueberries. By dawn, they were exhausted, but readied themselves as the leg-scratching cicada alarm was sounded. The ant army was approaching.

The ant army was divided into three columns and they converged on the tree from the west, south, and southwest. The armies could be recognized by their battle flags signifying the 1st, 2nd, and 12th army divisions. All in all there were thousands of ants in each division, not to mention the myriad of their allies—burly wolf-spiders with ant riders on the flanks, half-starved timber termites in the middle, and poisonous, prickly, leaf-cutting caterpillars near the front. The very front lines were reserved for the largest and strongest honor guard ants, which included the flag bearers.

From their platforms on the archer vine, Twig and Nut watched them advance. Above them were more archers.

"I wonder where three through eleven are?" Twig said with a nervous chuckle.

"What?" said Nut. "Three through eleven? There has to be thousands of them and you're wondering…"

"Never mind, Nut," interrupted Twig. "There's going to be one less anyway."

Twig fixed an arrow and beaded in on the flag bearer of the 1st army group that was approaching from the west. The shot was tremendously long, but Twig pulled back hard on the bow and released. The arrow arced high over the creek and found its mark in the thorax of the giant ant. The ant fell quickly, but the flag never touched the ground as another massive ant grabbed it and held it up firmly. The soldiers marching behind simply walked right over their fallen comrade.

"Nice shot, Twig," Nut said, and added, "but they do seem to get over it quickly."

"Let's see how quickly," said Twig, as he let fly another arrow. Again it sailed high into the air and landed in the center of the standard bearer, and again another took his place.

"Three's a charm," said Twig, as he shot once more. But this time when the flag holder fell, the flag dropped to the ground without a single ant offering to grab it. In fact, they formed a ring around it, each one staring at the other to see who was going to have the "honor." The entire 1st army group came to a halt; honor guard ant looking at honor guard ant. Some even turned to the termites, who wagged their antennas as if to say, "Nope, not me!"

Suddenly, the general screamed at a colonel, and the colonel yelled at a major, and the major pointed at a captain, who nudged a lieutenant, who prodded a sergeant, who grabbed an honor guard ant by the throat and forced the ant to pick up the flag.

"Forward!" the general commanded, and the column continued their march toward the tree. Nut chuckled.

"Ha! That was too much fun," he said, and laughed some more. "Did you see the way...?"

"There's nothing funny about death, Nut," interrupted Twig. "Not even an enemy's death." Twig paused, looked up at the sky and then back toward the advancing ants.

"Maybe we should simply leave now," he said. "Maybe Leaf's dad was right. We don't have to fight this battle at all. They have to stay on the ground. We could float out of here and…."

"And what?" said Nut, who looked at Twig to see why he had stopped in mid-sentence. Twig was staring into the trees across the creek, his mouth wide open. Nut looked to see what he was staring at and shuddered.

Across the way, from tree to tree and covering nearly every branch, were enemy hornets and flying red ants. The leaves weren't the only ones who could master the air.

It was unusually and depressingly quiet in Leaf's home. Leaf sat on the floor of his living room trying to get Stretch to leave him alone. Stretch was jumping onto Leaf and nudging his hand to get him to play, but Leaf was in no mood to entertain the insistent spider.

"No, Stretch!" Leaf whined. "I don't want to play right now. Stop it!"

Leaf's mom sat on the sofa deep in thought and Eric sat in his lounger holding Flower. Flower tugged on her dad's nose and ears and poked him in his eyes.

"Ow," Eric said pretending to be hurt. "That's my eye, you little eye poker," and then tickled her. She giggled uncontrollably.

"Stop it, Stretch." Leaf repeated to the persistent pet. "I'm gonna hurl you…"

"That's enough, Leaf," Eric said sternly. "Don't be mean. He's only a spider."

Stretch kicked with his legs as if to say, *"Yep, that's right,"* and then continued to goad Leaf into playing. Leaf shooed him away again and again.

"Stop it, Stretch!"

"Come here, Stretch!" commanded Leaf's mom. Eric and Leaf turned to her with surprise. She hadn't said a word since returning home. Stretch ran to her and leapt onto her shoulder. "And hand me Flower," she added to Eric.

"Why?" Eric asked. "What's wrong?"

"What's wrong?" she exclaimed loudly. "You have to ask me that? You are sitting there pretending nothing is happening, and Leaf is sulking on the floor, and you ask me what's wrong. The ants are going to attack, the tree is going to be cut down, the Colony is in danger and Thicket Figthorn is in charge. What's wrong? Eric Red Leaf, what isn't wrong?"

As she stood and snatched Flower from Eric's lap, the tears fell down her cheeks. Eric stood to follow her to the bedroom but there was a knock on the door. Eric opened it to Principal Oakreach and several other members of the council. Eric put his hands on his hips and spoke with a tone of resignation.

"If you've come to accuse me of anything more," he said, "you might as well…"

"We have looked at the map, Eric," the principal interrupted. "We have come to apologize."

CHAPTER FIFTEEN
ONE HOUR

The ant general ordered his emissary forward with a white flag of truce. The emissary, an old, fat ant who rode an even fatter caterpillar, slowly made his way through the ranks of the ants, timber termites and honor guard. As he passed the flag bearer on his left he leaned to the right—just in case—and nearly fell off, causing a chuckle from the ant lines. He righted himself, as if nothing had happened, and kept moving within a few feet of the nearest defensive wall. He unrolled a scroll to read the ant general's statement of demands.

"A proclamation of terms set forth this day and written on behalf of the glorious Queen Mother, Rotundra the 70th, by General Omar B. Little the 429th. I salute you who are about to dry!"

"*Die!*" yelled General Little.

"Oh. I'm sorry, General," apologized the emissary. "It's very hard to read. Okay then, I salute you who are about to *die!*"

"Thank you," said a voice from above. "But we intend to live!" The leaf who spoke from above floated down to the nearest branch. He held a large bow in one hand, a dozen arrows in the other, their shale rock tips glistening in the sunlight, and a quiver full of arrows hung on his back. On his side was a sword carved from buckhorn strapped in its sheath, and a knife made from conch shell was tucked into his tunic belt. His face was painted with light and dark green hues and he wore a brown bandana around his forehead. Thicket Figthorn was ready for war.

Behind him, hundreds of leaf archers outfitted in the same way hid amongst the regular leaves, waiting for Figthorn's signal.

"Our terms are simple," the emissary continued. "Surrender or be annihilated."

Meanwhile, Leaf and his father were hurrying down to the lower levels. Eric's spirit was renewed by the conversation with Principal Oakreach and the other council members. If Eric couldn't get Figthorn to change his mind about fighting, at least he could make sure the women, children and the elderly were in a safe place. The word had been spread—get everyone who wasn't fighting to the other side of the creek. Eric would get to Figthorn and tell him to stall the enemy until everyone was moved.

Leaf couldn't remember the last time he had hurled a gnarl or plowed through a V with his father, nor could he remember the last time someone had outraced him. Eric was ten spider legs ahead.

"Come on, Son!" Eric said.

"I'm right behind you, Dad!" Leaf yelled back and then had an idea to get there quicker. "See you there!" he said and did a dangerous maneuver—tucking and diving straight down the trunk. If it was executed properly, a trunk drop—as the movement is called—is a straight shot down and a win, if one is competing in a contest. If done incorrectly, one smashes right into a V and loses horribly. Leaf loved doing trunk drops. Eric couldn't bear to watch him.

Leaf sped down the trunk like a bug-eyed gerbil running from a hungry hawk. Left and right and right and left he avoided the V's and the smaller branches until he was almost to the bottom. He pulled up in time and grabbed the nearest vine in order to sling slung over to the lower branches. Unfortunately, the vine he grabbed was a defensive post that held thirty archers. The archers, including Twig and Nut, held on for dear life as the vine swung violently back and forth.

"Thanks, Leaf!" Twig called out sarcastically, while holding the vine with one hand and Nut with the other. Nut had fallen but Twig had caught him in time by the scruff of his neck. Leaf flipped up to give Twig a hand pulling Nut back on to the vine.

"Sorry, guys," Leaf said as he helped Nut. "I didn't see you."

Leaf looked down to see where Figthorn and the ant emissary were speaking. He scanned the ant armies and gulped.

"There sure are a lot of ants," he said.

"They've got termites, caterpillars and wolf-spiders, too. Check out the trees," Nut said.

Leaf saw the flying ants and the hornets and his heart sank. Then he saw his father land next to Figthorn.

"What's your dad doing?" Nut asked.

"He's going to stall their attack until the rest of the Colony can cross the creek. Listen, Dad wants us to take the *Flying Vine* down the creek and past the bend to the other side as well. He doesn't want the ants to destroy it."

"Let's go!" said Twig and Nut, and off they went.

Eric stood on the branch next to a very agitated Thicket Figthorn.

"What do you want? I'm in charge!" Figthorn said.

"I know, Thicket, but I…"

"Get back to your level or I'll have you locked up!"

Eric sighed and turned to the emissary.

"As you can see," Eric said, "we have a slight disagreement and need a little time to discuss the matter. Some of us want to fight and some don't. Could you give us an hour to decide?"

The emissary squirmed in his seat on the caterpillar. "I suppose I could ask General Little if…."

"We don't need time to discuss anything!" shouted Figthorn. "I'm in charge here, and I speak for the entire Colony!"

Eric leaned forward to whisper to Figthorn about the plan to stall, but Figthorn pulled away. Frustrated, Eric yelled, "One hour, Figthorn! One hour is all we need to make sure we are doing the right thing!"

"The right thing is to defend our honor!" Figthorn insisted.

"The warriors will defend, but what honor is there for the women and children and the elderly?" Eric asked, and then whispered, "Who will need time to get to safety!"

Figthorn finally understood what Eric was saying. Even though he and Eric had been at odds with each other, Figthorn immediately realized the need to get the non-combatants to safety, and secretly felt a tiny bit of remorse for not thinking of it sooner. He turned to the emissary. "Oh. I see. Yes, an hour should give us time to discuss things. Could we have one hour, please?"

The emissary shrugged his shoulders. "It shouldn't be too hard for me to…"

"No!" shouted the general. "I want your answer now!"

Leaf, Twig, and Nut caught air and headed toward the center of the defenses. Leaf had to do something he didn't want to do, but his father had insisted that he find Shady, Rake and Stump and get them to help sail the *Flying Vine.*

"But Dad," he'd said. "You don't know them like I do. They are trouble."

"Trouble or not, it's not a tiny, three-person craft," Eric had insisted. "You need their help. Maybe this is their chance to finally do the right thing."

Maybe, Leaf had thought, *but probably not.*

On the way up, the boys ran into Garland who was helping load food and other provisions from the main supply pantry and onto the back of a large, Hercules transport beetle. Several other beetles were already loaded.

"What are you guys doing?" Garland asked.

"We're looking for Shady," Leaf answered. "Have you seen him?"

"Right here, sport," Shady said, coming out of the pantry with an armful of supplies. Rake and Stump followed behind him doing the same. "We're working. What are you doing?"

Leaf looked at Garland and rolled his eyes and wagged his head.

"What?" Garland asked, and lifted her hands in the air. "Is there something wrong with us working together? It's not like *you're* helping."

"It's urgent," Leaf insisted. "We're taking the *Flying Vine* downstream. My father said…"

"Your father is not in charge anymore," Shady interrupted. "No one is taking the ship anywhere without my father's order."

"You want to try and stop me?" Leaf said.

"I'll thump you hard, tree-counter!"

Principal Oakreach ran into the fray to get between them. "Boys! Boys! That's enough!" the principal yelled. "The enemy is down below us and the council has agreed on some issues and one of them is to move the ship to a safer harbor. We need to work together. Now get going, please!"

The boys put their fists down and headed for the docks. The principal turned to Garland. "You had better go, too. They'll need someone with a level head."

CHAPTER SIXTEEN
BATTLE

"I think we should surrender," Eric said loudly enough for everyone to hear, even though he was speaking to Thicket Figthorn standing next to him. Figthorn played along.

"I would rather die than surrender," he replied.

"What good is it to die, when we know the ants will take such good care of us?" Eric asked and almost laughed. Figthorn actually chuckled.

"Then you should ask them to lunch," Figthorn said, and put his hand to his mouth to stifle a laugh.

Eric turned to the side so the emissary couldn't see his face. He was shaking with laughter and his eyes were watering. He struggled with each word, trying not to burst out hysterically. "I…..have…..a…..nice…..onion….. grass…..soufflé."

They turned their backs completely to the ant emissary, who stood dumbfounded watching the men shake. The emissary cleared his throat loudly.

"Eh hem! Um, so, ah, what is your answer?" he asked.

High above in the tree, a cicada scratched its legs to signal the all-clear. The elderly, women, and children were safe. Eric and Figthorn looked to each other and smiled.

"Here's our answer!" shouted the two men together and pointed to the branches above. "Fire!"

And with that, the archers revealed themselves and let loose a volley of arrows into the ranks of the enemy, and as quickly, turned around to hide themselves again. Hundreds of ants fell dead in an instant. The emissary squealed and prodded his caterpillar to back away from the onslaught but kicked too hard, lost his balance and fell to the ground. It probably saved his life. As he hurriedly crawled over the bodies of slain soldiers, the archers turned again and fired. This time they were joined by the catapults, and by the rock, acorn and javelin throwers.

A torrent of destruction fell onto the ant army that still stood in orderly ranks, completely taken off guard.

"Looks like rain today, Red Leaf," Figthorn said as the two watched from their perch.

"Hail storm, more likely," Eric replied, and then added, "We'd better get higher!"

As Eric and Figthorn caught air to the higher levels, the ant general lifted his hand and pointed toward the tree. "Attack!" he yelled, and then had his hand pierced by an arrow. He screamed so loudly in agony that all of the ants turned to look at him. He struggled to speak. "I....said.... attack!" The ant soldiers turned to the front and marched forward, but as they did dozens of poisoned blueberries landed around them. They broke ranks and the younger, less-experienced soldiers dove headlong into the treats faster than a parched mosquito slams into a bleeding raccoon. Blue-mouthed ants staggered and fell all over the battlefield. Others didn't even notice as they scurried to eat their fill. Soon they joined their comrades in wasp-venom death. Only the more-experienced soldiers and officers straggled past to join the front ranks.

In the front ranks, the ants approached the sticky-wall of spider webbing, and immediately got stuck on it as arrows, javelins, acorns, and rocks

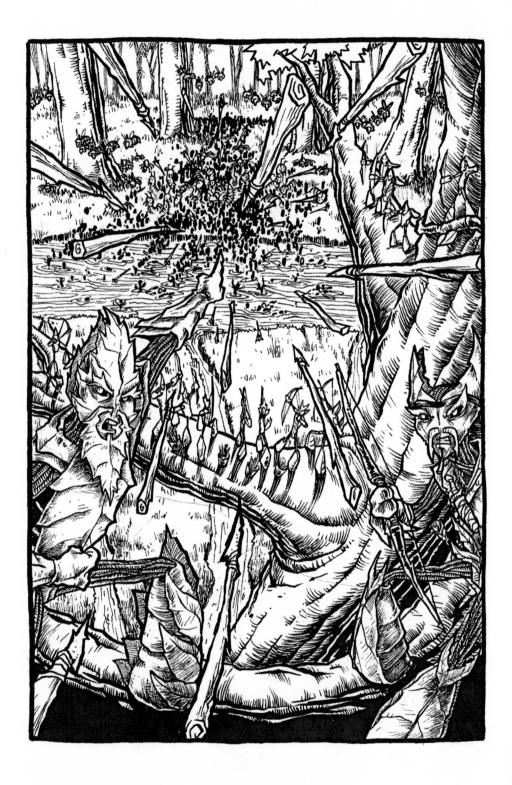

rained down on them from above and from the catapults. The acorns and rocks were especially effective as they bounced and rolled through huge chunks of ant soldiers.

On the ground in front of the tree, Wedge Raven was in charge of the squadron of sixty catapults, which were manned by more than two-hundred warriors. Wedge ran along the line of javelin-slinging catapults, urging the men to keep up their rate of fire.

"That's it, boys!" he shouted. "We're decimating them!"

Behind the catapults and closer to the tree was Wedge's second-in-command, Twig's father, Sap Twigford. Sap carried a bow and commanded a small contingent of archers and swordsmen to make sure the catapults were guarded from every angle.

"Keep steady, men," he cautioned. "Don't fire now. Keep an eye out on the flanks and watch for…." He cut his words short as a wave of flying red ants appeared over the ant lines heading straight for their position. "Air units!" he shouted, and pointed towards the enemy. "Air units!"

As flying red ants zoomed over the creek, the leaf warriors on the vines turned and fired, ripping a huge hole in their formation. The ones who were left were met by a hail of arrows from Sap's men. The air assault fizzled completely, with only a few ants returning to their lines.

"That's it fellas, that's it!" Sap encouraged.

"Good work, Sap!" Wedge said. "That ought to make them think twice about heading our way."

And it appeared to be so. The ants stalled in their attack and retreated back to their lines.

"Hooray!" the leaf warriors cried, and celebrated. Figthorn heaved a sigh of relief and tapped Eric's shoulder.

"See, Eric," Figthorn chided. "I told you we could take them."

Eric looked out at the thousands of ants that lay dead. By his counting there were at least one hundred more alive for every one they had killed.

"Yes, Thicket, we won this round but we're going to need a lot more arrows."

"So, let's go down and get the ones we already used," Figthorn said with a devious grin on his face. "They worked once and they'll work again."

Figthorn commanded one hundred archers to leave their positions, float down, and grab as many arrows as they could off of the dead ants. If they could do it quickly enough, and then catch air to return, the ant general wouldn't have time to order an air assault.

But what Eric and Figthorn didn't know was that the ant general couldn't care less. A few hundred arrows were nothing compared to his thousands of troops. Plus, he was busy making adjustments to his plan and quietly preparing a little surprise of his own.

Meanwhile, Leaf and his friends raced through the branches to get to the docks. They hurled the gnarls and plowed through the V's, oblivious to the battle raging down below. They were high enough up and on the far side of the action, and were only concerned with the competition of being the first to the *Flying Vine*. As usual, Garland and Nut had fallen behind.

Leaf was accustomed to racing Twig, but Shady was a different type of competitor. He pulled Leaf when Leaf was ahead, and pushed on him when he was behind. Leaf couldn't shake him. When there were vines to sling slung, Leaf and Twig would each grab one vine and leave one for the other, but now, as Shady got to the vines first, he grabbed as many as he could, hoping to slow Leaf down. It was working. Leaf was being out-raced.

Rake had some tricks, too. He didn't care if he was the first to reach the ship, but he was going to make sure he got there ahead of Twig. The two were neck and neck and, as they approached a break between branches,

Rake suddenly grabbed Twig and slammed him into the branch. The collision knocked the wind out of Twig, but he was able to grab a smaller branch to keep from falling. He hung there, catching his breath, as Garland and Nut approached.

"Are you okay, Twig?" Garland helped him to his feet and brushed him off. Twig looked at Nut, who appeared to have hit a few branches on his way as well. Twig gave a pained smile.

"It looks like I pulled a Nut," he said. "I'll be okay. Are you doing all right, Nut?"

"Yeah, I'm fine," Nut said as he straightened his helmet that had lopped over one eye.

"What are you guys doing?" Leaf asked, floating down to join them. He had returned, not wanting to race Shady any longer. He wasn't winning and it bothered him enough to convince himself that he needed to see where his friends were.

"We're resting," Twig said with a tinge of sarcasm.

"What are you doing back here?" Garland asked Leaf. "You sure seemed in a hurry to beat Shady to the ship." Leaf thought hard before he spoke.

"Sometimes you have to take responsibility for your actions and help those in need," Leaf said with a modicum of maturity. "You can't miss the forest for the trees, you know, and run off trying to win stupid races when your friends need you."

"Very grown-up of you," Garland said.

"Thank you," Leaf replied.

"Shady was beating the bark off you, huh?" Twig said.

"Crushing me," Leaf admitted. "He was pushing and tugging the whole way."

"The truth is," Twig conceded, "Rake pushed me into the branch."

"I figured. You're too good to hit it on your own." Leaf paused, and then added, "Sorry, Nut."

Nut took off his helmet and scratched his head. "Sorry for what?"

"Never mind."

CHAPTER SEVENTEEN
TO LANDS UNKNOWN

Seeing the slaughter that rained down on his troops, General Little decided he needed to do two things: take down the sticky wall, and keep his soldiers away from the blueberries. So, he did what any good general would do and improvised.

He had his soldiers work quickly to construct lightweight shields made from sticks and bark that were large enough to completely cover the tree-eating termites and the leaf-munching caterpillars. Then he placed his men on top of the termites and caterpillars to hold the shields. The ants who weren't riding were told to hold on to three-meter-long vines tied to the backs of the termites. Then the general did something very strange. He ordered all of his men to blindfold themselves. He reasoned that if they couldn't see the blueberries, then they wouldn't want to eat them. He knew they were too tempting a sight for his younger troops.

He instructed the termites to gnaw through and tear down the sticky webbing wall and make their way across the water to the tree. The riding ants would be protected from the attack above, and the ants in tow would be out of range until the assault could begin.

The second attack began with an air diversion. Three waves of hornets and flying ants flew high and out of range, and then dove down onto the archer vines. The archers repulsed them easily but their attention was diverted from down below as droves of shield-covered termites made their way to the wall to chop into it with their fangs.

Catapults fired hurriedly and the javelins effectively pierced the shields, but they weren't as accurate against the individual termite "tanks" as they were against masses of ants. Archers fired from above but the arrows bounced off the shields. The general ordered a giant wave of hornets and flying ants to attack the vines. The archers had to fight with their swords and hacked scores of them out of the air, but too many of the archers were grabbed from the vines and driven down to the ground on the enemy side of the creek.

Eric recoiled at the horrible sight. "Get the men up to the second level and focus on their air forces!" he shouted to Figthorn, but Figthorn was too busy shooting arrows. "Signal second level!" Eric ordered, and the cicada sounded the alarm.

Meanwhile, the termites had destroyed the sticky wall and marched toward the creek, joined by caterpillars as they pulled the vine-led ants across the creek. Wedge and Sap were sure the ants would stop to eat the berries. Many ants couldn't resist the thought of the blueberries and, orders or no orders, ripped off their blindfolds to dive into the water and eat their fill. Their lifeless bodies soon floated downstream. But the majority kept their blindfolds on until they were safely across.

As the ants poured across the creek, Wedge ordered his soldiers to catch air. Sap and his men covered their retreat as best they could until they were out of arrows and the ants were almost upon them. Sap ordered his men to the second level then looked to Wedge, who was busy trying to load one last shot of javelins into a catapult. An ant, the first to cross the creek, was coming at him quickly.

"Come on, Wedge, fly!" Sap shouted, but Wedge wasn't listening. As he loaded the last javelin, the ant reached him and bit his leg.

"Yeow!" Wedge hollered and then drew his sword to cut off the ant's head. The ant's head stuck to his leg as he crawled over to the catapult, but before he could fire it, Sap returned, grabbed him, and caught air as an endless stream of ants poured toward them.

"I wanted to fire one last shot," Wedge complained, as he pried the ant's head from his leg.

"Too bad, my friend," Sap replied. "It's better to catch air and fly away today and live to fight another day."

Eric and Figthorn watched from above and sighed with relief at the narrow escape, but their relief was short-lived. A squadron of hornets flew in quickly and grabbed Sap and Wedge and carried them away toward the enemy lines. They disappeared into the hordes of ants that covered the ground.

Figthorn screamed, "No!" and shot arrows wildly into the ants below. "Not Wedge! I can't believe they got Wedge." The warrior wiped a tear from his eye and then stiffened.

"At least they won't be able to climb up, eh, Eric?" he said. "It'll be too sticky." Eric looked down and discovered they were in more trouble than they thought. The catapults had been abandoned before they could be destroyed by Wedge's men. Eric realized they could now be used against them, and he watched as the general ordered the catapults to be turned around.

"They are going to fire themselves up and over the sticky part!" Eric exclaimed. And that's exactly what the ants did. Using the captured catapults, they flew up and into the air and landed above the sticky trunk. From there they dropped vine ropes down to the ground. The ants began climbing the tree and, unknown to the defenders, the enemy air forces had landed above them and were working their way down. It wouldn't be long till the leaf army was trapped in the middle.

On the other side of the tree, the kids floated down to the docks. They could see the *Flying Vine* resting in the calm water, but it was surrounded by what appeared to be floating debris.

"What's all that stuff floating around the ship?" Nut asked Leaf.

"I'm not sure," Leaf replied, "but it's coming from the waters around the tree."

"Dead ants," said Shady, matter-of-factly. "They've been floating here for a while—at least as long as we've been waiting for you 'slug slimes' to arrive."

Sure enough, as the kids got closer they could see the dead ants floating with either the blue from the blueberries around their mouths, or an arrow sticking out of their bodies.

"Yeah, looks like some of them took a berry bath," exclaimed Rake.

Shady and Stump laughed loudly. Nut chuckled nervously but then glanced toward Twig who was rolling his eyes. Nut stopped laughing and remembered Twig's words.

"Th...th...there's nothing funny about death," he said softly.

"What?" Shady said, not hearing, but then turned his attention to Leaf who had landed on the dock, and was running to jump onto the ship. Shady jumped on ahead of him.

"In case you were wondering who got here first," Shady reminded Leaf.

"I don't care," Leaf said dryly. They looked at each other for a second and then turned to the others and yelled at the same time.

"Untie the ropes and..." They stopped and looked at each other again.

"I'll be giving the orders!" Shady commanded.

"By what authority?" Leaf demanded.

"My father is in charge!" Shady asserted.

"So what? Your father has no experience!" Leaf fired back.

"Neither do you," Shady said. "So you won't take my command?"

"No. Will you take mine?"

"No," replied Shady, and then paused to look at Rake. "We'll make Rake in charge then."

"Impossible!" Twig shouted.

"Well, you're not doing it!" Rake shouted back.

The boys turned to Nut and Stump. The two of them shook their heads from side to side. They all paused for a moment and then looked to Garland. Garland was surprised but not overwhelmed by the thought.

"No problem by me," she said. "Actually, I couldn't think of a better compromise, or for that matter, anyone more capable." She looked to Leaf and added, "For now." She surveyed the ship and then her crew. She barked out orders with more command then Mr. Frostcone in the duel yard.

"Stump, untie the ropes! Rake, Twig, Shady, Leaf—man the oars! I've got the rudder, and Nut, you're on helm. Steer us out, and follow my commands!"

The boys stood there dumbfounded. No one moved. Nut was almost choking with anxiety at the thought of maneuvering the huge vessel. Leaf had never heard Garland speak that way, and Shady was totally perturbed by the whole affair.

"Move!" Garland yelled. "We don't have time. Hide the ship now!"

Stump untied the boat from the dock and hopped onboard. It was the quickest he had ever moved. Leaf, Shady, Twig and Rake looked at each other for another second and then sprang for the oars. Nut was the only one who didn't move. Garland went to his side.

"Don't worry," she whispered. "You'll be fine and I'll be right here with you to tell you what to do."

As Garland helped him onboard she glanced back at the tree. Unbeknownst to her, Leaf was doing the same thing from his position on the oar. They were both worried about their families.

Fifty yards north, in a quiet nestling of pine and beech trees, Leaf's mom sat gently rocking a crying Flower in her arms and softly humming a soothing melody. The words finally came to her – a song Eric had written while out to sea, but in expectation of his return to see his new daughter:

I didn't know what love could bring
Like snow that melts
Uncovering spring
I'd never known a daughter
You were just a dream

As the years went past
And hopes subside
The dreams at last
Had finally died
No daughter would come
No baby girl could be called mine

But an angel appeared
Saying let it be done
Together we'll pluck from heaven
The perfect one

And your eyes are hers

And your smile is mine
And the rest I guess
We'll know in time
My baby – as pretty as your momma
My baby – rest with your daddy
My baby – you cry and my tears are happy

I didn't know who you would be
A cross between
An angel and me
We sought you both together
In a waking dream

And we brought you here
Our little girl
Not knowing how
You'd fit in this world
The sands of time
Strand the most wonderful pearls

You're a cross between
Heaven and earth
You're a cross between
The past and a future worth waiting for

And your eyes are hers
And your smile is mine
And the rest I guess
We'll know in time
My baby – as pretty as your momma

My baby – rest with your daddy
My baby – You cry and my tears are happy

She stopped singing as Flower drifted off to sleep and looked around her to see several hundred other mothers with their children, along with elderly grandmothers and grandfathers, who all stared back in the direction of their home.

They had made their escape as quickly as possible, with transport beetles not only toting supplies but also carrying all of the elderly who couldn't catch air on their own. Mothers carried their babies, and the small children followed closely behind. They had gone out from the top levels on the northern side, hidden from the advancing enemy. She had helped organize the escape by going from group to group and telling them what to bring. Only the necessities, she told them, and then reminded them of what those necessities were.

"Don't forget blankets," she told some. "Not too many clothes," she told others. "Only take as much food as you need for tonight and tomorrow," she said to them all. "We can't load ourselves down with too much. We have to move quickly. What we don't have we'll either make or find. Come on now, we can do this."

Her words were encouraging and brought hope to all who had heard her. Even Principal Oakreach took a cue from her and made sure everyone was comforted. Once they had reached safety, he helped many groups settle in for the wait. Then he walked over to her as she rocked Flower.

"Your husband is a good man," he whispered to her, trying not to wake the baby. "And you are a fine leader yourself, Mrs. Red Leaf."

"Why thank you, Principal Oakreach," she whispered back.

"Please," he insisted. "Call me Oakley, Mrs. Red Leaf."

"Only if you call me by my first name," she said.

"And what is your first name, Mrs. Red Leaf?"

"Why, it's Rose," she said with a smile. "My name is Rose."

They both paused and looked back in the direction of the tree. Neither of them could even imagine what was happening back at the battle. They wished for the best, that the all-clear signal would come, but deep inside they carried the fear that all was lost. They could only hope their warriors could get away to join them. Living in the tree seemed much less important now than seeing the faces of their loved ones once again.

Eric stood on a branch on the tenth level with his sword in his hand. Surrounding him were hundreds of other leaf warriors holding their swords. They had long since run out of arrows. Below them on the eighth level, the ant armies had reformed their massive lines and were moving cautiously, yet steadily, upward. Termites led the way with wolf-spiders and their riders on the flanks. On the twelfth level above the leaf warriors, the hornets and flying ants swarmed on the branches looking to block the leaves from floating away.

"Let's charge their air forces," Figthorn said to Eric. "We can take them by surprise, work our way to the top and fly out of here."

"I'm thinking the opposite," Eric replied. "We should drop down to ground level and then catch air to get out of here. Maybe we can evade them and..."

"We'd still have to fight their air forces," Figthorn interrupted. "They are faster than we are, and we'd be better off fighting inside the branches then outside in the open air. They'll shred us out there."

Eric thought about it and, as much as he wanted to avoid fighting, he came to the conclusion that Figthorn was right. They had already lost many men, and it wasn't easy trying to figure out which way to go to minimize more loss. Eric was about to tell Figthorn that he was right when Figthorn ordered everyone's attention.

"Listen up!" he commanded. "We don't have much time, but I have to say what is on my mind and I have to do it now."

All of the warriors gathered closer so that they could hear him. Eric braced himself, not knowing what was going to be said. Figthorn spoke but had difficulty getting it out. His mind was full of the destruction of the day and of the loss of his friends.

"I want you to know that I was wrong," he said with a cry in his voice. "I wanted to fight for the honor of the Colony, and maybe for my own honor, but now since all may be lost, I only wish to see my family and friends gathered together in safety. We've lost too many men and I must resign from being in charge. Eric Red Leaf was right. We should have moved to safety while we could. The tree is just a tree. We could have gone to any…" He stopped and sobbed. Eric moved closer and put his arm around his shoulder.

"You are a brave man, Thicket Figthorn," Eric said, "and you are a fine warrior. The Leaves of Old would be proud."

"Here! Here!" the other warriors called out. Figthorn composed himself and turned to the men.

"I didn't finish what I wanted to say," he said. "I suggest we ask, and I might even beg, for Eric Red Leaf to return to leadership. All in favor say 'Aye'!"

"Aye!" the men yelled.

Eric didn't have time to fathom the whole turn of events. Rightly or wrongly, whether he wanted to make it or not, the next decision he made could very likely be his last. It could spell doom for all of the warriors. As the ant ground forces approached the ninth level and their air forces moved to the eleventh, he thought of his family and was glad that at least they were safe. He took a deep breath and issued the order….

"Row, Leaf!" Shady shouted angrily.

Leaf snapped out of his thoughts and realized that he wasn't doing his job. The ship was barely moving with only four rowers, and with his attention elsewhere, only three of them were giving it their all. The *Flying Vine* was built for forty rowers—twenty for each side—and could handle a crew of seventy-five plus cargo. It was huge.

We're barely drifting, Garland thought, and then realized that Stump stood idly by after untying the ropes.

"Stump, you take Twig's place on the oars! Twig, you climb up to the crow's nest and keep an eye out!" As the boys ran to their stations, Shady turned to Leaf and groaned.

"She sure is taking her position seriously," he whispered to Leaf.

"Why shouldn't she?" Leaf replied.

"She's a girl," Shady said.

"So, girls can't be serious?" Leaf asked. Rake, who was sitting behind the two, chimed in.

"They don't know nothing about leading things," Rake said.

"You mean they don't know *anything* about *leadership*?" Leaf corrected.

"Exactly!" Shady and Rake agreed as if the matter were settled. Leaf rolled his eyes.

"I guess we'll see, won't we?" he said.

The late afternoon sun was beginning to lose its beams in the heart of the forest, and there were only a few spots of light remaining on the water. Shadows already covered most of the creek. With Stump's help, the ship moved a little faster. Garland worked the rudder to guide the ship out into the center of the creek. The current was stronger here and they picked up a little speed. The plan was to move around the first bend and moor against the other side away from the vision of those in the tree. Twig sat atop the mast in the crow's nest, looking back in the direction of the dock. He started to yell down that all was clear, when he spied movement in the air around the lower levels.

"Hey, guys," Twig said as quietly as he could. "There's something coming and…" He stopped when he saw what it was.

"What is it?" Shady yelled up.

"Shhh!" Twig implored.

"Don't tell me to…" Shady responded but was cut off by Garland.

"Quiet!" she said as softly and sternly as possible. "You'll give us away."

It was too late. A squadron of hornets, ten strong, came in low and bore down on the ship quickly. They had heard the oars splashing loudly as the boys were desperately trying to get the ship to move. Shady's voice had been confirmation that something was on the water. When they had spied the ship, they'd headed for it with abandon.

"They see us!" shouted Twig to the others. "Get armed!" As Twig shouted he realized he didn't have a weapon. *This is not good,* he thought, and then ducked down low in the crow's nest, hoping not to be spotted.

As Leaf and the other boys jumped up they saw five of the hornets land on the ship, while four others circled above. One headed back toward the tree, obviously, Leaf thought, to report back to the general. The hornets perched on the railing and drooled with delight at finding the ship manned merely by children.

"Surrender now," said the flight leader, "or end up stung like your papa's back at the tree."

The thought that their fathers had been hurt or killed struck deep into their leafy hearts, but it hardened their wills and made them even more determined to survive. Stump grabbed an oar, as did Leaf; Shady

and Rake had their sling-shots. Garland was the only one with a sword and she placed herself between the hornets and Nut.

"You had better get off of my ship," Garland commanded, and held up her sword, "or you'll be the ones getting stung."

The hornets smiled maliciously and their stingers pulsated and dripped with venom in anticipation. They jumped down from the railing, and as the closest hornet approached the boys, Stump swung his oar and knocked the hornet into the water. Shady and Rake fired their slings and two more of the hornets fell dead, their huge stingers still shaking on their lifeless torsos.

The hornet leader signaled the four who were circling to come down. They landed behind the group much closer to Garland and Nut. Garland lunged at one but it took off and hovered out of reach, laughing at her. His delight was cut short as Shady nailed him with a rock.

Two other hornets went after Garland and she swung at one and then the other to keep them at bay. The third got behind her and went for Nut, who stood frozen in fear. As the hornet was about to lunge, Twig zoomed down from the crow's nest and landed on its back with a thud. Before the dazed hornet could move, Twig grabbed its wings and shredded them with his bare hands. It writhed in agony, flopping around on the deck yet still trying to thrust at Twig with its stinger.

In the meantime, as Garland continued to fend off the two hornets,

Leaf ran to her rescue. He clobbered one with his oar and when the other one looked his way, Garland slashed it with her sword. That left the leader and one other hornet near the stern of the ship facing Stump, Rake and Shady.

"You fight pretty well," the hornet leader said to the group as they all approached him with oars outstretched and sword and slings at the ready. "But you can't fight and row at the same time." As he spoke, he looked in the direction they were floating.

It was then that the kids turned and realized the current had taken them down the creek and that the *Flying Vine* was heading for the Northern Branch. None of them had sailed that far before, but they knew of the rapids they were quickly approaching.

The hornet leader laughed and quickly ducked as Shady and Rake aimed their slings and fired. Rake hit his target, sending one hornet into the water as the leader flew away.

"I'll be seeing you again soon," he said, and headed back toward the tree.

"Quick!" Garland yelled. "Everyone on the oars!"

But as the ship plunged into the Northern Branch, the quicker current violently tossed the ship and its occupants like a rag doll in the hands of a preschool Acorn. The *Flying Vine* was flying out of control and the kids could do nothing to stop it.

CHAPTER EIGHTEEN
TAKEN

Rose Red Leaf sat in the darkness feeding a hungry Flower a small snack of burl nuts and mushrooms. She wanted to make herself eat, figuring she would need the energy, but her stomach was in no mood to make the space. Her nerves were on end and a sickening despair was grabbing her from within and choking her leafy veins.

It had been hours since they had made their escape; the all-clear signal had not been sounded, the men had not sent any word, and Leaf and the other children had not returned. Close by, other women were sobbing and children were calling out for their fathers. Rose sighed and hugged her tiny daughter. As she pressed Flower against her chest she heard a squeal and realized that Stretch was in her top pocket. She had placed him there quickly in her rush to gather the few belongings she would need to make her and Flower and Leaf more comfortable as they waited for the men.

"Oh, my!" she said and helped him out. "I'm so sorry, Stretch." Stretch sat in her hand for a moment, looked himself over, and then flexed his legs to make sure nothing was amiss. Satisfied that all was well, he jumped down and landed on Flower's shoulder and hugged her. She cooed with delight and said, "Setch!"

Rose smiled and was grateful for the short distraction from her fears.

She needed to plan the next day's itinerary for the refugees. But as her ideas took shape, she chided herself for even thinking them.

Eric will be back, she thought. *He'll be making all the plans for us, you silly. There's no need for you to worry.* She paused and then her mind considered, *But what if he doesn't make it back? What if he's delayed or hurt or even…?* She stopped herself and willed her mind to think positively. She needed to be strong for her daughter and for the rest of the Colony. *The "rest of the Colony",* she almost scoffed at the thought. There's not much of a Colony left. *Where is my man? Where is my son?* Her mind was about to drift into despair again when she heard a welcome sound—leaf warrior voices. The men had returned!

All along the branches of their make-shift home, men's voices softly called out to their families and in response the women and children called back. The joyful sound of the reunions spread quickly from level to level.

Rose hurriedly put the food away, tucked Stretch back into her pocket, and stood clutching Flower with anticipation. She peered into the darkness expecting to see Eric in each small group of men that approached. He was not among them. In fact, there were many men missing. Cries of anguish could be heard as the women questioned the men about loved ones and were then reluctantly told the harsh truth of their demise. Rose, fearing the worst, hardened herself to find out Eric's fate. She approached the last group to land—three men struggling to carry a wounded warrior.

"Wh…..wh….where is Eric Red Leaf?" she stammered.

The men stopped in their tracks and bowed their heads, each waiting for the other to speak. Rose waited and bit her lip. Despite her own urgency, she was in no hurry to force someone to tell her bad news. One of the men, the youngest of the group, approached her and looked her in the eyes.

"Ma'am," he said. "I'm afraid he was taken." Rose felt like she had been kicked in the stomach. Her knees buckled and she would have lost her grip on Flower if the man hadn't braced her and helped her regain her balance. He sat her down on the branch as she cried. And then almost as soon as she began to cry she stopped. A thought had crossed her mind, and she struggled to speak.

"Taken?" she said. "Taken, how? What do you mean by taken?"

The man cleared his throat and sat down beside her. He was obviously exhausted by the events of the last twenty-four hours. He had helped with the defensive preparations the night before, had fought the long battle during this day and night, and had his nerves on edge the whole time. Rose handed him some water and he gulped it down.

"Thank you," he said, and wiped his mouth and chin. "This isn't easy to say, and there are some things I don't know, but I'll do my best to tell you exactly what happened." Rose hugged little Flower tightly as the man spoke. Stretch squealed again so she took him out of her pocket and set him on her shoulder.

"We were trapped on the tenth level," the man continued. "The ants were coming up from the ground and coming down from the air. We were out of arrows. Thicket Figthorn called us together and apologized for making a mess of things, by pressuring everyone to fight. I can't say I didn't want to fight, or that I felt pressured at the time, but looking back I think we might have made some better choices." Rose knew exactly what the man was talking about.

"Anyway, Thicket stepped down from leadership and called for your husband to lead us again." Rose's heart jumped a little, knowing that Eric had been vindicated and that even if it were his last act, at least he was respected by those he led.

"The plan," he said, "was for us to charge their air forces above, and at least avoid the bulk of their army. If we could punch through, then we'd have a chance of escaping." The man hung his head as he spoke the next words. "We lost quite a few, but we'd have all been taken if not for Eric Red Leaf and Thicket Figthorn."

Rose wasn't so much concerned with how the two men had saved the rest but what the word "taken" meant. The warrior continued his story before she could ask again.

"First, your husband asked the ants for a moment to discuss surrender terms. He said the ants love it when you admit defeat." The man chuckled and Rose gave a faint smile. "He wanted the sun to set, figuring their air forces would calm down a little as the night air cooled and that the darkness might aide us in evading them. Finally, when the ants ran out of patience, and called for a decision, we formed a V and shot up through the branches, stabbing and hacking as we went, but there were so many of them. The hornets and flying ants swarmed all around us and were trying to hem us in long enough for their ground forces to catch up when Eric broke ranks to a side branch and yelled, 'I'm the leader of the leaves! You can't take me!' The enemy jumped at the opportunity to get him, but there were still so many around us. Thicket Figthorn then went in the opposite direction and yelled, 'No! *I'm* the leader! Come and get me!' So many hornets and ants flew after him that most of us were able to break out of there and make it here. Your husband and Thicket Figthorn were taken by the ants and hornets. I didn't see exactly where they took them, because I was fighting, but the last thing I saw was the two of them being led away to the lower levels. I'll never forget what they did, ma'am."

Even though Rose wiped a tear from her eye, inside her heart a small glimmer of hope prevailed that Eric was still alive. Instinctually, she rehearsed the coming morning's instructions to the survivors. Like it or not, they were going to follow her to safety, and she was going to discover a way to find her husband.

CHAPTER NINETEEN
DARK CLOUDS

Garland sat on a small rock overlooking a calm pool of water surrounded by trees. In this section of the river, beautiful wildflowers grew along the banks, butterflies and dragonflies danced among the blooms, frogs jumped in and out of the water and ducks landed from above to wade, bathe, and eat from the water vines. It would have been an idyllic scene, straight out of a forest daydream, except for the nearby wreckage of the *Flying Vine* and the six, half-drowned boys lying sprawled in the rocky sand several feet away from her. She sighed. Never in the history of sailing, she thought, has a ship been captained for less than an hour before it met with total destruction. She sighed again and yawned. She was more than exhausted. She was totally drained both physically and emotionally.

The night before had been harrowing. After the hornet attack, the kids had tried as best they could to guide the ship out past the Northern Branch and through the rapids, but they didn't know the course through the rocks and they certainly couldn't find it in the dark of night. The ship was furiously jarred, but had successfully emerged through each layer of the rapids until it finally hit the biggest rock of all and shattered apart at the seams. The group held on to anything they could grab and rode the river the rest of the way to the pool. They had all been bumped and bruised by the long ride and had spent more time flailing under the water than they did floating on top. Garland seemed the least scathed, and had helped each one of the boys make it to shore. It hadn't been easy moving them, and next to impossible moving Stump, but somehow she had managed.

Garland saw that Leaf was the first to stir. He sat up and immediately put his hand to a large bruise on the right side of his head where he had hit a rock. His right shoulder also ached so he switched hands, found that to be uncomfortable and collapsed back down and moaned. She went to his side.

"Hey," she whispered. "You okay?"

"No," Leaf said, and looked up at her. He could tell that she was tired and he felt awful for being a burden, but he couldn't even will himself to get up. "Sorry for not being much help."

"Don't worry about it," she said, and glanced over at the other boys who remained motionless. "At least *you're* awake." She held him in her arms, and as she cradled his head, softly sang a song her mother had taught her whenever she was hurt or upset:

Calm is the water
Soft is the sun
Caressing gently
Everyone
Sweet are the breezes
Garden grown
All around
Our forest home
Summon the clouds
Oh come and see
The wonders shown
For you and me
Calm is the water

Soft is the sun
Caressing gently
Everyone
Summon the clouds
Oh come and see
The wonders shown
For you and me

Leaf drifted off to sleep again as she sang and dreamed of fluffy white clouds floating through the air. He watched them as they swirled, changing their shapes in the wind. Horses danced and rabbits twirled. Flowers bloomed and wilted and then bloomed again. The wind blew the clouds some more and they became silly smiling faces that turned from side to side, saying at first "hello" and then "good-bye". And then all at once the clouds appeared to be looking down toward the ground, searching for something or someone. Suddenly, they spotted what they were looking for and circled back to take a closer look. They hovered together with one purpose and then dropped toward the ground with lightning speed. The sound they made was deafening, high-pitched and resounding, like ten thousand wings beating the air. They came nearer and nearer to a spot by the river, and there, sleeping in the sand was….Leaf shuddered in his sleep. The clouds were descending upon him! Still dreaming, he closed his eyes, not wanting to see, but when he looked again, the sky was black; the sun totally obscured by hornets, their barbed stingers coming closer and closer. They were only inches away when Leaf willed himself to awaken and then jolted upright.

"What is it?" Garland asked Leaf. "Is my singing that bad?"

"Yes," Rake said from nearby in his sandy bed. "I thought someone had caught a swamp rat by its tail."

"That's not funny, Rake," Shady said, gazing up at the sky from his prone position. "She can sing to me any day." He stood up and turned to

see Leaf in Garland's arms. "Oh," he said. "Your singing is good but the company you keep could do with a little…re-tuning."

"Very funny," said Garland, who then noticed Twig and Nut stirring in the sand, and Stump waking up from the base of a tree.

"You boys okay?" she asked, as the three got up and dusted themselves off.

"I guess so," Twig said and walked toward Garland and Leaf. Stump grunted something, but Nut didn't say a word. He was in a daze, walking in circles and mumbling to himself. He looked faintly better than the beached debris of the *Flying Vine*, only dryer.

"Help me up, please," Leaf said while holding his head. Twig helped Garland lift Leaf to his feet.

"We have to go," Leaf said.

"Go where?" Shady said as he walked toward Leaf. "And who put *you* in charge now?"

"Yeah, I thought Miss Swamp Rat was in charge," Rake added and laughed.

In a flash, Garland unsheathed her sword and ran at Rake, but she swooned from exhaustion and fell into Shady's arms. He gently laid her down in the sand. Leaf ran to her and knelt down.

"Get away from her," he said to Shady.

"She came to *me*," said Shady.

Leaf was too hurt and too worried about Garland to pay Shady any attention. There was ringing in his ears and it reminded him of the buzzing wings of the hornets.

"Twig," Leaf said. "Come here quick, and help me carry her into the tree line." The two brought Garland to her feet, and despite the complaints of Shady and Rake, they all made their way to the trees. Stump heard the sound first and gazed up into the air.

"You guys hear that?" he asked. The others looked up not knowing what to make of it, but Leaf knew.

"Hornets!" he said. "Follow me this way!" Leaf quickly led them deeper into the woods. As they hid behind a tree, they could see the hornets; more than a hundred of them flying along the course of the river, looking this way and that way for the ship. Thankfully, the wreckage of the *Flying Vine* was no more than sticks and twine and was spread out amongst the natural tree limbs and other flotsam found floating near and upon the shore. The hornets didn't notice and kept on their path.

"That was close," said Shady, who then turned to Leaf. "How did you know they would be coming?"

Leaf thought for a moment and then smiled. "I heard it when Garland was singing...*to me*." He paused long enough for the last two words to sink into Shady's brain. Shady grunted and walked away.

Garland sat with her back against the tree. She felt a little better, although a little embarrassed as well. She didn't like showing weakness and she sure didn't like showing that kind of anger toward Rake—even if he did deserve it.

"My turn to apologize," she said to Leaf. "Now *I* don't seem to be much help."

"Don't worry about it. We'll carry you down to the bay if we have to."

"Down to the bay?" Garland said. "We need to get back home."

"I don't think we have a home anymore."

CHAPTER TWENTY
HEADS OR TAILS

Eric woke and for a few seconds couldn't understand what was going on. The ground seemed to be moving underneath him, but it also seemed to be taking him along with it. As he came to his senses he realized that he was being carried. His arms and legs were tied with vines and he had been blindfolded. Something was carrying him; something that was both soft and prickly at the same time. Had he been there, Nut would have known exactly what it was. Sure enough, Eric was being toted by an entire squad of wolf-spiders. *At least I'm not dead,* he thought.

Only a few hours before that Eric would have thought otherwise. As he stood upon the branch and shouted for the hornets and flying ants to come at him so that the others could escape, he was amazed at how quickly they surrounded him and carried him off. He took a few bites and several stings before going unconscious. His last thought was that he was glad his family was safe and that the other warriors were able to break free. Darkness then enveloped him.

He wondered now how far the journey would be before he got to the queen. It would probably take a couple of days and maybe he would have a chance of escaping. He checked the tightness of the vines around his wrists and ankles. They were firmly tied. He relaxed, partly because there wasn't any use in exerting himself, and partly because his wounds were aching. He couldn't decide which was worse, the stings or the bites. He'd been stung twice in the back and once in the neck, and the hornet venom throbbed, but the ant bites in his arms and legs were debilitating as well. *I wish I could spit,* he thought.

"Attention!" an ant messenger said ahead of him. "Camping in one hour, check?"

"Check!" the ants replied from all around.

"Two days more to Elkhorn!" the messenger said. "Check?"

"Check!"

Check that, Eric thought. *Put me down, go to sleep and I'm out of here. I don't want to arrive at Elkhorn.* As he thought about what Elkhorn must be like, a voice called out nearby.

"Eric!" the voice said. "Eric, can you hear me? Are you there?"

Eric was about to respond when the caller howled in pain. Thicket Figthorn was being scolded for talking. Eric remained silent, but now knew that he wasn't alone.

As the ants set up camp, the wolf-spiders quickly dug two holes into the ground and deposited Eric and Thicket in them, and then covered them up to their necks with dirt. Two ant guards were placed nearby. One of them removed Eric's blindfold and he was finally able to see Figthorn. Figthorn on the other hand was buried facing away from Eric. Eric waited till the guards weren't looking and whispered.

"Hey, I'm right behind you."

"Great," Figthorn said. "Glad to know you've got my back."

"I can't see your back," Eric said and chuckled, "but your neck looks red."

"Yeah, a giant flying ant bit me. Would you mind?"

"Not at all," said Eric and proceeded to try and spit onto Figthorn's neck. He missed, though, hitting him in the back of the head.

"Thanks," said Figthorn. "I needed to wash my head. Got any soap?"

"Let me try again," said Eric, and then froze as one of the guards hurried over quickly and opened his jaws as if to bite him on his face. The guard stopped his bite in time and said, "Shhhh! Quiet or you won't have a mouth."

Eric nodded and then swallowed.

At dawn the next morning, the wolf-spiders dug the two out and set them on a root of a nearby elm. Their wrists were unbound, but their legs were still tied tightly together. Their bodies were numb from inactivity, so they quickly rubbed themselves to get the circulation going and then spit into their hands and applied the spit to their wounds. Immediately, they felt better. The ant guard from the previous day walked over and threw a chunk of brown, red, and purple meat at them.

"What's this?" asked Figthorn with disgust.

"Breakfast," said the ant.

"Smells like stinkbug," said Figthorn.

"Actually, it's worm tail," said the ant. "Or it might be worm head. You know how hard it is to tell which end is which?"

"Head or tail, no thanks," said Eric, "I'll pass, but thank you for your kindness."

"Oh, don't thank me," said the ant. "If you don't eat the house specialty, then your friend will be added to the menu. It's the least I can do for such an appreciative leaf-loving vegetarian."

The ant laughed harshly at his own joke, stepped over toward Figthorn and pulled out a sharpened stick. He grabbed Figthorn by the foot and leaned him back into the root of the tree. As he was about to slice off Figthorn's foot at the ankle, Eric reached down and grabbed the worm meat and took a bite.

"Ummm, delicious," Eric said while chewing.

"Here, give my friend some, too. He'll love it."

The ant smiled and took the meat from Eric's hand, but Eric quickly grabbed the ant's other hand, took the stick, and sliced off the bindings around his legs. The ant yelled for help, and lunged toward Eric, but Figthorn rolled off the tree root and kicked the ant away from Eric with both legs. Eric quickly cut Figthorn's bindings and the two of them caught air as the ants scrambled to grab at them. Fortunately, there weren't any flying ants or hornets at the camp, so Eric and Figthorn could make a clean getaway. But as they rose with the air current and floated over the ant camp, they spied some familiar faces staring at them from their holes in the ground. Wedge Raven and Sap Twigford were about to receive their morning's breakfast of worm tail. Or maybe it was head.

CHAPTER TWENTY-ONE
THE RIVER

That same morning, Rose was having a difficult discussion with herself over what the next step was going to be for the Colony. *Moving wasn't the hard part,* she thought, *but knowing where to move to was a different matter.* The ants had come from the south or maybe the southwest. They wouldn't be hard to follow, but it had to be done very carefully. She had to assume they still had their air forces. *We'll head south,* she decided, *and follow the course of the river.* Then she had a change of thought.

Maybe we shouldn't move at all. Maybe we should wait till the kids return. What if they come back and we aren't here? Several of the warriors had gone down to scout along the water's edge, but hadn't seen any sign of the ship or of the children. They also reported that the ants seemed to be gone.

The kids must have gone downstream, she thought. *So, we'll keep an eye out for the ants and for the kids at the same time.* With her mind settled, she got busy gathering up her things. Principal Oakreach approached her with a familiar looking tube in his hands.

"Let me guess, Oakley" said Rose. "That's a map."

"Yes, Rose, it is. You are very astute."

"Thank you."

"You are welcome," he said, and pulled out the map from the tube. "Here's the map made by my great-grandfather, Oakley the Reacher."

"Good," said Rose. "We'll need it once we leave the course of the river."

"The river? The ants didn't go that way."

"I know," said Rose. "We're going after the kids first. We'll send a few scouts out to follow the ants. Once we know the kids are safe then we'll go after the men."

"That must have been a tough decision," said Oakley.

"The toughest," said Rose.

The two of them stared at each other for a moment and then Rose turned to pick up her belongings. When she turned back around, Oakley could see that tears were rolling down her cheeks, but her eyes were ablaze with defiance.

"We're going to need lots of arrows, Oakley. I mean lots. Instruct everyone who is able to start making them and to keep making them all along the way. I want what's left of the Colony, from great-grandfathers to Bloom-aged girls, armed with bows."

"You got it," Oakley said. "We'll put out a call to the birds to bring their feathers and ask the squirrels to make stick piles along our route. Anything else?"

"Yes," Rose said. "I wish everyone to pray."

The caravan of old and young set off almost immediately as word spread that Rose was in charge and that they had a purpose. Scouts floated toward the Northern Branch that led to the river. A separate band of five warriors started off to follow the ant trail. Transport beetles carried the elderly, the infirmed and wounded warriors, and mothers carried their babies. Rose led the way, with Principal Oakreach by her side and fifty warriors close behind. Rose had wanted to have Flower with her, but had

been talked out of it by the principal. She didn't want to agree, but he had made a strong argument.

"She'll be fine with Nanny Barkbottom," he had said. "She loves Flower like her own, and if you are going to lead all of us, including the soldiers, you may have to react quickly. Having a small child in your arms will cause you to hesitate."

It wasn't long before they made it to the river. The stillness of the morning had given way to swift afternoon breezes that were to their backs. The transport beetles were especially happy about that. The Colony turned south to look for the children and the *Flying Vine*.

As they floated, they also stopped to gather up the stick piles from the squirrels and feathers from the birds along the way. Word had spread quickly of the ant attack and of the needs of the Colony. Squirrels also left bundles of nuts, roots, mushrooms and seedpods, and the birds gathered berries and edible flowers. Although the transport beetles were not especially happy about the extra provisions, they figured they'd get to eat, too, even if they did have to carry the brunt of it.

While most everyone shaped, sharpened, and fletched arrows, Rose searched the shoreline for some sign of the missing children. There was nothing but the trees and the river. She gave a worried look to Oakreach, who pulled out the map.

"There are bad rapids further downstream," he said. "They were supposed to put to shore at the first safe place away from the tree."

"Maybe it wasn't safe," she said. "Maybe they were followed and had to keep going."

The sky darkened earlier than they expected as clouds moved in from the west. The wind picked up and made travel difficult and very dangerous. As large drops of rain began falling, Rose looked to the trees for shelter. She picked a spot that was past the worst rapids and where the waters emptied into a beautiful pond full of fish and frogs. The dragonflies and butterflies had already sought refuge from the storm. The ducks were gone, too, but for an entirely different reason.

As they set up a make-shift camp to protect themselves from the wind and rain, a cry went out from ladies gathering sticks along the shoreline. The wreckage of the *Flying Vine* had been found.

CHAPTER TWENTY-TWO
IT'S ALL OVER THE FOREST

After the hornet squadron flew south to follow the river, Leaf and the others skedaddled their way through the trees to the southern end of the pond, where the river flowed out again to make its way to the bay. The going was not easy. Thick foliage and vines blocked their passage, and they dared not catch air for too long so as not to be spotted.

"This is insane!" shouted Shady. "Why we are going this way and why we are going so slowly is beyond me. I vote we head back to the tree."

"I second that," said Rake who plopped himself down in the sand.

The rest stopped and sat down on rocks near the shoreline. Stump was huffing and puffing for air.

"I…ah…I…ah…I third," he finally got out.

"I'd fourth," said Garland, "if it made any sense to *fourth*, or even to agree—but I don't."

"Why not?" whined Shady. "What can we accomplish by going to the bay?"

"We have to find a new home," said Leaf. "The Coastals know where one is. My father…"

"Oh, here we go again," said Shady, "The trees are…."

"They are leaving soon," interrupted a voice, which turned out to come from a duck swimming nearby. The duck spoke quickly and had a nervous habit of dunking her head under the water between sentences." *Dunk.* "If they leave they won't come back for a long time, and you won't get to go." *Dunk.* "I once took a trip to a pond on the other side of the forest, and if it wasn't for a gaggle of geese, I wouldn't have made it back." *Dunk.* "Why do they call it a gaggle?" *Dunk.* "That's a strange word, don't you think?" *Dunk.* "It makes me choke to think about it." *Dunk.* "Gaggle!" *Dunk.* "Hmmph!" *Dunk.* "It should be a 'geegle' or a 'goosle' or a 'flockle' or a…."

"Thank you, Ms. Duck," Garland interrupted. "But who is leaving soon?"

"She is," said Rake, who loaded a rock into his slingshot and drew back to fire. "She's driving me crazy with her babbling and dunking." Twig quickly stepped between Rake and the duck to block his shot.

"Put that down," said Twig, but Rake didn't budge.

"Don't tempt me," said Rake. "I'd much rather plunk you instead."

Garland looked to Shady, who smiled and motioned for Rake to lower his slingshot. Rake grimaced but did it anyway.

"You boys finished?" said the duck. *Dunk.* "Your army is crushed, your men are captured, you lose your home, you wreck your boat, you're being hunted by hornets and I come over to help you and you want to hit me with a rock?" *Dunk.* "Are you insane?" *Dunk.* "You sound like a bear I once met, who wanted to eat me after I spent an entire afternoon trying to help him catch a fish." *Dunk.* "It wasn't my fault his big ole paws couldn't hold a slippery…"

Leaf interrupted, "What? What happened to our army and to our men?"

"You don't know?" said the duck. *Dunk.* "It's all over the forest." *Dunk.* "I heard it from a wren that stopped to drink here." *Dunk.* "She heard it from a squirrel who heard it from two chipmunks that were burrowing in the dirt near a…"

As the duck finally got around to telling the kids about what had happened back at the tree, Leaf's idea of going to the bay seemed to be the last thing they should do. His mother and the rest of the Colony were looking for them and his father was a captive. Shady stood up with his hands on his hips.

"I told you we needed to get back!" he said. Leaf silently agreed, but it was Garland who spoke. She turned to the duck.

"You said they were leaving soon. Who is leaving soon and how can you help us?"

"Ahhh," said the duck. *Dunk*. "I wondered when you would ask." *Dunk*. "I once told a beaver that he was building his house near a nest of water snakes, but did he listen?" *Dunk*. "No!" *Dunk*. "He was half-way through building when…"

Garland interrupted the duck. "Please tell us, who is leaving?" she asked.

"The people of the bay are leaving soon," said the duck. *Dunk*. "They are going to explore the new land." *Dunk*.

"When?" asked Leaf. "How do you know?"

"Soon," said the duck. *Dunk*. "They are preparing their ships and they are very excited about it." *Dunk*. "Apparently, they talk about it all the time." *Dunk*. "The rats heard them and told us and actually teased us about it, saying that if we got to go on the trip, we'd simply be 'dinner.'" *Dunk*. "Stupid rats!" *Dunk*. "They'll take a ride anywhere and not even think about whether or not they'll have any food." *Dunk*. "I think they eat their own…"

"And how can you help us?" interrupted Garland.

"My friends and I could give you a ride." *Dunk*. "I once gave a ride to a moth that had a bad wing," *dunk*, "but he got wet, because I'm wet, and if you've ever seen a wet moth it's not pretty," *dunk*, "because they kind of stick to themselves, or to anything really, and he, well let's say he didn't really need to go anywhere after that because…."

And so, as the duck continued to talk, six of his friends swam over and carried Leaf and the others downstream. When they came to a small area of rapids, the ducks flapped their wings and took off into the late afternoon sky. As they headed south, they didn't know that a little ways ahead of them the hornet squadron had tired of their search and were heading back north.

CHAPTER TWENTY-THREE
THEY'RE GONE

Eric and Figthorn were feeling good and bad at the same time. They were happy to be free from the ants but frustrated over not being able to rescue their friends. As the ants continued their march to Elkhorn, the two followed the column cautiously from tree to tree for hours, not knowing if the air forces would return. Had they known that the ant general had flown back to the queen with the flying ants, and that the hornets were searching for the kids, they might have been a little bolder. But figuring that two being free was still better than four being captive, he and Figthorn kept their friends in sight but remained hidden themselves. It was the best they could do.

"Let's get in there when they camp tonight, Eric," Figthorn said.

Eric didn't answer. His mind was a million miles away and time was racing by in a vision of the past. He thought of Rose and Leaf and Flower and all the times he had left them home to launch off on expeditions. The countless months and years he'd spent at sea became weeks and days and minutes and seconds that slowly slipped past like a ship heading toward a horizon on a never-ending sunless morn. He regretted every moment apart from his family. Figthorn looked to Eric to speak again and then noticed the tear that rolled down Eric's cheek. He stopped himself and gazed into the distance in the direction where Eric was looking.

"I've missed the forest for the trees," Eric finally said. "I thought duty and honor and responsibility, and leading the people and defending the tree and finding a home, were the most important things that I could do, but I was wrong. There are much more important things. When you're a husband and a father, you need to be engaged in the lives of your family. What good is it if you work hard for a future and you're not even around for the present? I wanted so badly to prove that I was right that I forgot why I needed to be right. Thicket, I never want to leave my wife and my children again."

The two leaf men continued to gaze out into the forest as the sunlight faded and the shadows deepened. Birds were playing their late afternoon games, and deer were foraging for dinner.

"It's easy to miss the forest for the trees," said Figthorn. "I look and all I see are..."

Figthorn stopped in mid-sentence. Eric turned to look at him and noticed his mouth was wide open and his eyes had a look of disbelief.

"What's wrong?" Eric asked.

Figthorn didn't answer right away. He blinked his eyes a few times, rubbed them with his hands and gazed harder into the darkening twilight. "They're gone," said Figthorn.

"What's gone?"

"The trees are gone."

The two men left the ant convoy behind and skirted their path to move closer ahead to where Figthorn was looking. Sure enough, ahead of where the ants were marching a wide swath of trees had been chopped down near a place where two roads intersected. Smoke rose up from the chimneys of the houses in a village west of the road to their right.

Eric and Figthorn caught a breeze up above the trees to see the village

in its entirety. It was large—larger even than the village by the bay. It had some forty houses and two main roads with several smaller roads that led to farms around the outskirts. They could see the many fires and candles burning as the darkness settled in.

"Now I understand, Eric," Figthorn said. "The Coastals aren't *coastal* anymore."

"It's getting dark," said Eric. "We'd better get back to the column. They've probably camped already."

The two tucked and rolled back the way they had come, hoping that it hadn't gotten too dark to see the ants. Luckily, the moon had risen over the trees and gave off enough light that the two leaves could find the trail of the ants. They didn't follow it long before they heard the chatter of the guards "checking" their night commands.

"Keep an eye out up above," said one.

"Check! Watch above," said another.

"Sound the alarm if you hear or see anything," said one.

"Check! Sound alarm."

From the first level of a tree above the guards, Figthorn chuckled. "Check, check, check."

Eric laughed softly. "They sure are efficient."

"Where do you think they're holding Wedge and Sap?" asked Figthorn.

"I don't know, but their efficiency gives me an idea to help us find out."

"What's that?" asked Figthorn.

"We'll need one of them to help us," Eric said.

"Oh, sure, we'll ask one of them to join us."

"Of course," said Eric. "He really won't mind if he's dead."

As Thicket Figthorn scratched his head, Eric floated down to the nearest sentry. As it turned out, the sentry was simply dying to help.

CHAPTER TWENTY-FOUR
DUCK DUCK GOOSE

Nut was unbelievably happy. You'd think that he would be terrified of this new turn in their adventure, but in fact, it was the opposite. Floating up through the branches on his own was one thing, but riding on the back of a flapping duck was another. He didn't have to worry about hitting anything, losing his way, or looking foolish. Even though his duck was the last in the line, he didn't care. He'd finally found his element and he felt like singing. He wanted to sing so much that he made up his own new song and sang it loudly for all to hear.

I can't believe my eyes
But I know it's the truth
I'm flying oh so high
That I'm gonna hit the roof
Come on, come on, come on and follow me
To the bay by the sea
I'm a leaf on the loose
Sing'n duck duck goose
Yeah, I'm a leaf on the loose
Sing'n duck duck goose

And with the last "goose" he yanked a feather from the duck's back-side and yelled, "Yahoo!" The duck jolted, kicked his wings into overdrive, and sped past the rest of the pack like they were swimming circles in a pond. Nut looked back at everyone with a big smile on his face and sang loudly again. When he got to "the bay by the sea" part, the duck turned his head around and said, "You can sing till the morning for all I care, and I'll still keep you in the lead, but if you pluck me again, I'll dive down into the deepest part of that water to eat a fish….and I hate fish!"

Now, Nut understood the old saying, "You shouldn't pluck the wings that fly you," but he did keep on singing. He sang it six times all together— once for every bend in the river. He was getting ready to sing it again when the hornets came out of the trees after taking a break to eat their lunch. They almost missed the duck's passengers, but the singing got their attention. They sprang to action and headed for the ducks. Nut yelled back to the pack, "Hornets!"

The hornets were closing in fast and it looked useless to try and out-fly them. Leaf yelled to the ducks, "Barrel through them and head for the trees," he said. "We'll hop off and rug out."

As the hornets flew up, the ducks dove down, and sliced right through all one hundred of them like a bolt of lightning through a honey-comb. Hornets went flailing and spinning in every direction. The ducks continued down to the tree line and the riders flipped off and hurtled into the lower branches of the first tree they encountered. Then the ducks took a hard left and landed safely in the river. Leaf went a little ways into the tree, grabbed a branch and froze. The rest followed his lead. As the hornets descended they flew right by the rugged-out kids. They searched and searched but couldn't find them. Even as it got dark, the kids continued their ruse until the hornets gave up and flew back up the river. No one dared speak until they heard a voice singing faintly near them in the darkness. "I'm a leaf on the loose…singing duck, duck, goose." They all laughed, left their hiding places, and came out into the open. Nut was the first to arrive.

"Let's find the ducks," he said enthusiastically.

"Let's rest for the night," said Shady.

"Well, for once I agree with Shady," said Leaf. "I don't think we have far to go. From the maps I saw in Principal Oakreach's office, I remember it wasn't far from the bends in the river."

The kids found their resting places and drifted off to sleep. The next morning they awakened to several noises they had never heard before. The first was a "chunk" sound that reverberated up through the trunk of the tree and out to the branches. The second was like a bear snoring, only faster and came from a little ways away. The third sound was the sound of Coastal words. They were loud words, harsh and strong. Leaf and the others rose quickly as the "chunks" became more numerous and made the tree shake violently. As they searched for the source of the sound, a human voice screamed out, "Timber! Timber!"

It was at that very moment that the leaf children learned some new lessons. The first lesson was in understanding the Coastal language. They soon learned that "timber" is what the Coastals say when the tree they are chopping down is ready to fall. The other new lesson was how to survive when your bed falls thirty levels in five seconds.

As they floated over to a large bush, pausing a moment to get their wits about them, they watched as the Coastals ignored the tree they had just chopped down to simply carry their tools over to the next victim to begin hacking and sawing.

Shady turned away from the forest and let out a gasp. What he hadn't seen the night before—what none of them had seen—was the devastation of the woods that stretched from where they sat all the way down to the bay. Trees had been felled by the hundreds, and what was once green and lush and full of life was now barren, except for silent tree limbs lying motionless on their sides like long-shed snake skins drying up and withering away in the early morning light.

"There are five Coastal settlements surrounding the forest," said Leaf. "Imagine how many trees are already gone."

Shady was speechless. Rake and Stump tried to get him to talk, but he was at a complete loss for words. He kept turning his head from the bay and then back to the forest over and over again, trying to grasp the magnitude of the destruction and to calculate how long it would take for the Coastals to make it to their tree. Finally, with a heavy sigh, he turned to Leaf.

"Sorry," was all he could say, barely audible, and forced.

Leaf nodded, stood up, and caught air.

"Let's get to the ships."

CHAPTER TWENTY-FIVE
A NEW QUEEN

The ant guard was unguardedly sleeping. He had pulled guard duty five consecutive nights without a break and that included the battle. He'd guarded the column as it marched to the tree, he'd guarded the supplies during the battle, and now again he was guarding the column on its way back to Elkhorn. He was so asleep that Eric had to wake him.

"Check," Eric said. "I've got another prisoner for you."

The guard woke up with a start and found he was staring into the eyes of Eric Red Leaf. He wanted to sound the alarm, but then saw the ant soldier who held Eric in check. What the guard didn't know was that the ant soldier wasn't alive, he was being held up by Thicket Figthorn, who was tied to the back of Eric. The two leaves blended together perfectly into a back-to-back leaf. Thicket mimicked the voice of the ant soldier and made the ant's mouth move by tying a stick to the ant soldier's jaw like a puppet. In the darkness, the ant guard could only see Eric and the ant soldier and the ant soldier's mouth moving. Thicket mimicked the soldier again.

"Where are the other prisoners being held?" he said. "I'll take this one there."

"Check," the ant guard said. "To the left of that tree." The ant quickly pointed in the direction they should go. He was only too happy to oblige since he wanted to get back to sleep as soon as possible.

"Check," Thicket said and pinched Eric to start moving. It worked perfectly. The two moved past the guard and through the throngs of sleeping ants. They rounded some large roots and came to the side of the tree, where they saw their friends who were buried neck deep and guarded by another sleeping guard. Sap Twigford and Wedge Raven's eyes lit up when they saw Eric, but then quickly dimmed when they saw the dead ant who didn't look dead.

Thicket coughed and woke up the guard. "The general is meeting the column in an hour and wants to see the prisoners. Dig them out now, check?"

"Check!" the guard said, but as he said it the stick that Thicket used to hold up the dead ant and make him talk suddenly snapped. The dead ant fell...dead—again. The ant guard opened his mouth to yell, but Eric grabbed him by the neck and squeezed. They struggled a bit, until the ant couldn't struggle anymore, and Eric turned around. Both Sap and Wedge gasped when Eric turned and Thicket suddenly appeared before them to start digging the pair out. Thicket smiled.

"Surprise," he said. Sap and Wedge simply stared with astonishment at the turn of events and at seeing both men together—literally. It didn't take long to free both sets of leaf men and deposit the ant guards into the unused holes.

They caught air and that's when the trouble started. The ant general really did return—and he had a large flying ant escort.

"Get them!" commanded the general from his perch on the back of the biggest flying ant. "I promised the queen. Now, get them!" His voice squeaked a little bit due to his fear of not keeping his promise. The flying ants, almost one hundred of them, sped straight for the four leaf men, who were trying desperately to catch a breeze, but the wind wasn't blowing. As ant ground forces climbed every tree in the area to get at them, and the air forces surrounded them, the four men's hearts sank. The ant general smiled.

"I told the queen I had four of you, and by my good antennae, I will deliver you to her throne!"

"I may not be a queen," said a voice in the darkness from above, "but my throne is the forest and your antennas are trespassing!" In an instant an arrow flew from above and sliced through the general's good antennae, splitting it and making it dangle down to his belly like his other one.

"Fire!" said the voice, and arrows flew through the air, downing nearly all of the ant air forces in a single volley. Rose Red Leaf and her band of leaf warriors, wives, mothers, grandfathers and teens caught air and surrounded Eric, Figthorn, Sap and Wedge. Together they all floated out of sight and into the trees.

When they felt they were safely away, Eric put his arms around Rose. Now it was his turn to have a look of astonishment on his face. She smiled and snuggled into his arms.

"Thank you," he said. "I think 'queen' is far too incomplete as a title for you."

"We think so too, Eric," said Principal Oakreach, who was floating next to them. "If you are still stepping down as our leader, then we plan on nominating Rose. She took care of us and organized us, and it's about time our Colony was led by a female."

"I second that," said Figthorn. "Either way, we'll have both of your input, and from what I've seen in the last few days, you both have everyone's well-being in mind."

As the group met up with the elderly and those who had looked after the small children who had been hiding safely in a large tree, Wedge Raven and Sap Twigford floated over to Eric and Figthorn. They both had worried looks on their faces.

"So when are we going after our kids?" asked Wedge.

"Yeah," said Sap. "Were they captured? Are they hurt? What are we going to do?"

Eric looked at Figthorn and Figthorn looked at Principal Oakreach. Oakley turned to Rose.

"Well now, gentlemen, you'll have to ask our new leader," he said.

Rose smiled nervously and said, "Hand me that map of yours, Oakley. We are going to the bay."

CHAPTER TWENTY-SIX
I HAVE A PLAN

Leaf watched the people of the bay from an apple tree in the garden of an old woman who had a dog. The dog knew that Leaf was there and circled the tree and barked and was generally very annoying, reminding Leaf of the stray bark beetle that had followed him on a Wednesday morning not too long ago. In fact, the whole scene reminded Leaf of the Colony, only on a larger scale: adults busied themselves with work; their children played, and animals worked, played, and protected. Although Leaf was astonished at how big everything was in the Coastal world, his thoughts turned to Stretch and wondered how he was doing and, of course, his mom and dad and baby sister. It had been a long journey down to the bay and Leaf hoped that somehow he would return to his family with some news that would be beneficial.

So far, the best thing he had found out was that the ships being readied for the voyage were still in dock. How much longer before they sailed he couldn't guess, but there was a lot of activity as men came and went and came again to load supplies.

As Leaf watched, Garland and Shady joined him on the branch. The dog went nuts and the old woman came out of her house to see what was wrong. She gazed up at the tree branch, saw leaves blowing in the breeze and nothing else. She yelled at the dog and walked back inside. Shady took aim at the dog with his slingshot.

"Don't you dare," said Garland. "It's a silly little animal."

"I'm practicing for the rats," said Shady, who continued aiming and then let loose a shot. He missed by two feet.

"Why don't you start with a bigger target like the house and work your way down," chided Leaf.

"He moved," said Shady.

"He moved his tail," said Leaf. Shady loaded his sling again.

"Move your tail and I'll show you…"

"All right, boys!" said Garland. "That's enough. We have more important things to worry about." She turned to Leaf. "Is there any plan?" Leaf stared at her blankly and sighed.

"I thought not," she said.

"I have a plan," said Shady.

"Really?" said Garland.

"Yes," Shady said, and then paused for effect. Leaf squirmed.

"Well?" Leaf asked.

"It's easy," Shady said. "We can't stop them from going, and we have to go back and get the rest of the Colony. We don't want to sail for who-knows-how-long to find new land and then not know how to bring everyone else with us. What if they sail to this place and never return? We'll never see our families again. The only thing we can do is to slow the Coastals down from leaving."

"How?" asked Leaf. "Shoot all their pets?"

Shady smiled sadly at Garland.

"Oh, he's such a petty, petty, silly boy, isn't he?" Shady said. Leaf wanted to thump him. He rolled his eyes at Garland, but she was too busy waiting for an answer.

"How do we slow them down?" she asked Shady.

"What will they absolutely not leave without?" Shady asked slyly. Leaf responded in a split-second.

"Charts."

"Exactly," said Shady. "We steal their charts."

"We *borrow* their charts," said Leaf.

"No, boys, we *hide* their charts," Garland corrected. "We don't want to risk them seeing us floating away, and besides, they'll be too heavy. Let's get some rest before the sun goes down. I think we're going to have a busy night."

Meanwhile, back at Elkhorn, the queen ant was in a rage and issuing orders faster than a cricket shaking its leg on a lonely night.

"Get me another general!" she commanded. "I want one with antennas that point up! Send scouts to follow those leaves that took my prisoners! Tell the hornets to track down those kids! Tell the wasp king he owes me a favor for stopping last summer's spider riot. They were going to turn his paper nest into confetti! Tell him I want transports for my army! I have a plan! If what that duck told me is true—and I know how to get the truth—then we need to get to the bay and get there fast! Now, move!"

As she shouted orders, couriers sped out of the throne room and straight to the flying ant terminals where flyers were readied to carry her orders abroad. She placed her hands on her rotund stomach and stretched it out to twice its size like a bullfrog croaks its throat. "And will someone please bring me more duck sandwiches. The first ten were delicious."

CHAPTER TWENTY-SEVEN
ALL ABOARD

Through the darkness, Leaf could barely make out Nut's silhouette back on the dock. Nut had lookout duty on one end of the dock and Stump was on the other end—somewhere. From where Leaf stood, at the top of the ramp on the ship, he couldn't see Stump at all. *He must be hiding superbly,* Leaf thought sarcastically, given Stump's size. *Or he's sleeping.*

Twig was stationed at the bow of the ship and Rake was aft at the stern. Leaf, Shady, and Garland waited for the lookouts to signal with their fireflies. Nut was first and gave the all-clear, waving his sticky glow-stick, which Curly Longroot had invented eons before by covering a stick with tree resin and then placing captured fireflies onto the stick. Six or eight fireflies on a stick are enough to send a signal on even the darkest of nights. Leaf signaled back to Nut and then looked again for Stump, but Stump could not be seen.

Leaf didn't know it, but he wouldn't have been able to see Stump, even if the big fellow was on fire himself. Stump had lost his fireflies while he practiced waving his stick. He'd rattled it so hard the lucky lightning bugs flew right out of the resin and away into the night, so Stump was busy skedaddling around the far side of one of the dock buildings searching for more fireflies. And to make matters worse, he was so upset, he was mumbling to himself. This was a problem, because unfortunately, he wasn't the only one searching around the dock buildings. Several rats were scavenging for people food and saw Stump.

"Shady's gonna bop me. He's gonna clobber me for sure."

The rats stopped in their tracks and watched as Stump scurried around swiping at fireflies and mumbling to himself.

"Eh, mate," said the first rat. "What's that and what's it doing?"

"It's a leaf," said the second rat, "and it's blowing in the wind, you ninny."

"No," said the third rat. "It's a leaf and it's talking to itself while trying to catch fireflies."

"Why would it want to catch fireflies?" asked the first rat.

"And since when can leaves talk?" asked the second rat.

"You never heard of the great leaves of the old forest?" said the third rat. The other two rats stared blankly. "They are the rulers of the wood, the kings of the trees. They subdued the hawks and they eat owls for breakfast."

"Really?" said the first rat.

"I like them already," said the second rat. "I'm scared to death of hawks and owls."

The third rat laughed and clicked his tongue. "You ridiculous rodents!" he said. "You think I've ever seen a talking leaf before, let alone one that looks for fireflies? Why is he doing this? How can he do that? How would I know, you ninnies?"

But it wasn't long before they found out. Stump finally caught four lightning bugs and hoped they would do the trick. He quickly headed for the other side of the building to his place on the dock and waved his stick. Leaf signaled back and the rats saw the whole thing.

"They're raiding our ship," said the first rat.

"We'd better tell Big Cheese," said the second rat.

"I wonder what they taste like?" said the third rat, and then the three headed back to their den to tell the others.

Right after Stump's signal, Leaf, Shady, and Garland started searching the ship for the charts. There were many large containers on the deck that hadn't been emptied or moved to the hold down below, and some smaller ones around the oars. They searched each one and then looked all around the helm.

"Nothing!" said Shady with disgust. "This is a waste of time. Charts are always in the chart room down below."

"I didn't expect them to be up here," said Leaf. "But I wanted to see what they were taking and how they were storing their supplies. We may need…"

"We may need to get out of here," interrupted Twig, as he came running from his lookout position. "Stump and Nut are heading this way fast and I thought I saw the ground moving this way, too."

"What?" said Garland. "Is it ants?"

"No, bigger." said Rake, as he came skedaddling over from the back of the boat. "A lot of something is coming fast!" The group ran quickly to the ramp and peered into the darkness back toward the dock. They could barely make out that Nut and Stump were frantically flipping and floating their way to them, and that behind them a shadow was growing and moving up the ramp.

"Oh, rats," said Leaf.

"Why?" asked Shady. "What is it?"

"Rats!" exclaimed Leaf. "They're rats!"

Nut and Stump both came aboard unceremoniously, slamming into the group of kids as they landed. Leaf and Twig were able to catch Nut and help him land, but Shady and Rake were knocked to the ground by Stump.

"Rats!" shouted Nut.

"Lots of rats!" shouted Stump.

As the rats came up the ramp, Leaf looked up and saw there wasn't any use catching air to go up into the mast. The rats would simply follow them up the ropes and the timber.

"We have to get out of here," said Garland.

"I agree with her for once," said Rake.

"No," said Leaf. "I'm not leaving here without the charts. Let's get in the hold and lock ourselves inside."

"And then what?" asked Shady. "Ask them to let us leave?"

"Maybe," said Leaf. "We'll figure it out once we have the charts."

The kids skedaddled their way to the hold's hatch, jumped down inside, and closed the hatch behind them as the first wave of rats hit the deck. Luckily, Garland had grabbed the two glow sticks that Leaf and Twig had dropped a moment before to catch Nut. She used them to light the hatch so Leaf could bolt it from the inside, and then they started searching for the charts. As the kids looked around, the rats came to the hatch. When they found it locked they banged on it with their fists.

"You'd better let us in," said one. "Big Cheese won't be very happy."

"None of you seem very happy, anyway," said Shady. "What's going to change?"

"The change will be," said Big Cheese, who was twice as large as the other rats and had pushed his way through the throng to the hatch, "that me darlin's might only add one of you's to the salad bar if they find that you's don't taste so good." The rats surrounding their leader hooted with laughter.

"Trust me," said Leaf. "We don't taste good. We only want to get something from here and then we'll be on our way."

"What could talkin' leaves from the forest want from inside a boat?" asked the leader.

"We want the charts to see where the people are going," said Leaf.

The leader laughed long and loud. The other rats chuckled, too, but didn't know why.

"Them charts ain't inside the hold, me little garnish," said the leader.

"I was about to say that," whispered Garland to Leaf. "They aren't here."

"So, where are they?" Leaf asked the leader.

"Oh, no," said Big Cheese. "It's nor that easy. What might I be gettin' in return for tellin' you's their location?"

Leaf thought long and hard. And while he was thinking, Rose and the rest of the Colony arrived on the dock. Had it not been for their finding Nut and Stump's glow-sticks, they might never have checked the ship. As they floated over the ramp, they saw the horde of rats gathered around the hold.

"I guess I can offer you all of the food that's down here," said Leaf to the rat leader. "There are barrels of grain, boxes of fruit and a ton of vegetables. Your salad bar should be tasty enough without us."

"All right, then," said Big Cheese, who had no intention of truly making a deal. "Come ye out and I'll tell you's where to find them charts."

"Oh, no," said Leaf. "Tell us where the charts are first then we'll open the hatch so you can have the food."

"That'll be fine, me little leaf, sir," said Big Cheese, who grinned evilly and then signaled to his men to catch the leaves when they opened the hatch. "You strike a hard bargain and I dare say you's have me word that I won't eat narry a one of you's." The kids could hear the other rats chuckling. "Them charts be in the captain's quarters in the village."

"He won't let us go, Leaf," whispered Garland.

"She's right again," said Rake, who readied his slingshot. "I'll plunk him full of so many holes they'll be calling him, Big *Swiss* Cheese!"

"I'll even take you's there, me self," said the leader. "It's the least I can do for such honorable tree relish, um, I mean tree fellar's." His men snickered again. "As a matter of fact, I'll even go and get them charts fer you's."

Meanwhile, Rose had decided to hide her people on the far side of the ship away from the dock. They lined the rail from bow to stern with arrows at the ready. They listened as Big Cheese made his offer and heard Leaf in response. Eric whispered to Rose.

"They are trapped down there," he said. "It might be good to attack now before the kids come out. That way they won't be in danger." Rose considered Eric's words and thought them wise. However, she wasn't convinced an attack was necessary. *Perhaps,* she thought, *the rats would scurry away if faced with a bigger danger.* She quickly organized her fellow leaves.

What Big Cheese and his band of rats saw next made them want to jump right out of their furry, flea-bitten skins. Rose and the rest had joined together and formed themselves from top to bottom into the spitting image of two of the biggest people they had ever seen, and seemed to rise up from the side of the boat. In the darkness, all the rats could see were two looming shadows coming at them faster than a flyswatter to a fly. The two giants were yelling, "Get off my ship! Get off my ship!" The rats screamed in horror and headed for the ramp. Eric dropped down from his position as one of the "people's" hands and knocked on the hold's hatch.

"Hey, buddy!" he said. "You can come out now."

Leaf recognized his father's voice and opened the hatch. With big grins on their faces, he and the rest of the group came out onto the deck.

Leaf squeezed his dad tightly and they would have had a grand reunion, but for the arrival of the ant queen and her army who were on the dock and blocking the rat retreat at the bottom of the ramp. The rats stopped dead in their four-legged tracks as they faced one thousand ants, three-hundred hornets, and two-hundred wasps. They hissed and bared their fangs and swiped toward the ants with their claws. The wasps and

hornets took one look at the horde of rats and at the two giants coming behind them and took to the air.

"Where are you going?" shouted the ant queen.

"We're out of here, lady," a wasp responded. "We were only contracted for transport. Good-bye, *Your Majesty!*" The wasp bowed low in feigned respect and then he and the rest of the wasps and hornets headed back north.

Big Cheese smiled, but then remembered the threat from behind. He nervously looked back at the ship and saw that the two giant "people" had suddenly transformed into hundreds of leaves with bows and arrows pointed straight at them. Rose got ready to order an attack against the rats and the ants, but Leaf came to her side and stopped her. He approached the rats.

"What's this then?" said the rat leader to Leaf. "Would you be a tryin' ta scare me's away from me food in the hold?"

"No," said Leaf. "I told you we only wanted the charts, but now that our families have arrived, we don't need them anymore. But we do have something you need."

"Don't listen to him, fat boy," said the ant queen. "They fooled you once and they'll fool you again. Now get out of my way."

"*Fat boy?*" said the rat leader and then scratched his belly with his claws. "And jest what would you's be want'n, me bee-less grounded pet?"

"We want the leaves," the queen said. "And I'm not grounded." She waved her hand and five hundred flying ants zoomed down from the roof of the dock building. Rose gripped Eric's hand tightly, wanting desperately to order the archers to fire the first salvo, to at least better the odds. Eric whispered, "Let Leaf try."

"And, after she's through with us," said Leaf to the rat leader, "she'll start with you and take all of your food. Her army is large and their hunger knows no bounds."

All of the ants licked their lips with anticipation of what this discussion of "food" implied. They hadn't realized how hungry they actually were until Leaf mentioned it. The rat leader squirmed a bit and then rose up on his haunches. He turned to Leaf.

"You said you's had something I might be a need'n, me leafy friend?" he said.

"Fight with us and all of the food is yours," said Leaf. "You have my word and I keep my word. You know you've seen ants eat your food before—but when have you ever seen leaves eat your food? We're on your side." And with that, all of the leaves took positions on the railing and aimed at the ants.

"It's a deal," said Big Cheese, and this time, he meant it. He turned to the ant queen. "Nobody calls me *fat boy* and then takes me own food. It just aren't respectful."

Eric squeezed Rose's hand.

"Fire!" shouted Rose and two hundred arrows felled two hundred ants in an instant.

"Attack!" shouted the ant queen, and her ground troops ran up the ramp while her air force headed for the archers.

"Charge!" shouted Big Cheese, and his rat army clawed and bit their way through the center of the ant line.

At first, the rats made good progress and pushed back the swarming invaders, but it wasn't long, though, before they were overpowered by the sheer mass of the teeming insects. Rats were completely covered in ants and went delirious from bites all over their bodies and faces—especially their long snouts.

The flying ants outmaneuvered the leaf archers, who, though they were firing furiously, couldn't keep up with the winged throng that engulfed them and mercilessly chewed on their arms and legs.

As the sun made its presence known over the eastern horizon, Leaf's perspective changed from an overwhelming involvement in the rapid movements of the battle, to a seemingly slow motion spectator position as if he were removed from the action. He looked to his father, who was busy hacking at three ants in front of him and at two behind, and watched as his mother shot arrows wildly at the wily ant flyers. He saw Garland grab Nut and throw him behind her as two ants came lunging at his acorn helmet. He observed Twig shoot two ants with one arrow, and he saw Shady and Rake firing their slingshots and Stump using his bow as a club. He saw Thicket Figthorn, Sap Twigford, and Wedge Raven fighting furiously as twenty ants surrounded them. He saw Principal Oakreach holding off a voracious ant flyer with his bare hands while another ant was readied to chew his leg. He saw the rats begin to fall back from the onslaught of the ant attack, and he saw Big Cheese covered in blood from the massive amount of bites he had taken. His head spun and he thought surely this was the end of his family and friends and the end of the Colony.

As he gazed up at the sky a shadow passed within inches of his face. He put his hands over his head expecting a collision, the sting, and the swirling descent into the depths of death. A moment passed and then he heard a strange sound. Cheers. There were leaf cheers and rat cheers and panicked cries from the ants. He heard a word he hadn't expected to hear—"Victory!" someone shouted. "Victory!" It rang out again and again. He heard his father laugh and his mother cry with joy, and then Garland was by his side.

"She's here!" she said.

"Who?" was all Leaf could say, but Garland didn't hear him. She was too busy screaming, "She's here! She's here!"

Time seemed to speed back up to reality. There was a flutter and the shadow that had passed overhead took form as a bird landed on the railing next to Leaf. Leaf recognized her immediately—the red-breasted robin whose young had been taken by the ants. Behind her, the rest of the robins chased the ants into the bay, and around the dock, and into the village. As she straightened out her ruffled feathers, Leaf could tell she wanted to speak, but she had something in her mouth. She opened it so he could see the ant queen inside.

"It was the droopy-antennae general that took your eggs," the queen screamed, her voice cracking and echoing from inside the robin's beak. "I didn't order him to do it! It wasn't meeeee!"

The robin chomped a bit and then swallowed.

"Sorry, Leaf," she said. "I was taught it is not polite to speak with one's mouth full. Mmmm, that was a queen fit for a meal!"

Leaf would have laughed, but he was still in shock. "How did you…I mean, when did you…I mean, why did you…."

The robin chuckled some more and spread a wing around Leaf's shoulder. "I once said I wished there was more I could do. Sorry it had to take so long." Two little robins landed at her side, still gobbling the last remains of several ants.

"These are my boys," she said. "If it wasn't for you, I would have lost them."

Garland couldn't contain her joy and had to hug one of the boys. The little fellow looked at her oddly at first and then leaned into her hug.

"I knew you before you hatched," she said. "I carried you for a little while—I mean, one of you, anyway."

"Thank you," he said. "I'm Garl, and this is my brother Lee."

Garland and Leaf shared a glance and then looked at the mother robin.

"You didn't?" Leaf said to the robin.

She shrugged her wings and admitted, "You did save their lives, didn't you, Leeeeaf and Gaaaarland?"

They all had a laugh and the boys gave Leaf and Garland big hugs.

"We are humbled you named your boys after us," said Garland.

"It is quite an honor," Rose said as she approached the group while leading a limping Principal Oakreach on one arm and a wounded Eric on the other. "Thank you for rescuing us all." Leaf saw the blood running down his father's forehead and down his cheek.

"Dad!" he shouted, and ran to help him.

"It's looks worse than it is," Eric said, as he hugged his son.

"That's what bandanas are for," said Thicket Figthorn as he came up behind them, "and spit." He spit on the wound and then rubbed a bit of the saliva onto the top of Eric's head. "That's for the shower you gave me back at the ant camp," he laughed and tied his bandana around Eric's wound.

"I feel better already," Eric said and laughed.

"You leaves are a strange bunch," said the robin.

"Yes, but we get along," said Rose.

Their attention was suddenly diverted as Rake, Twig, Nut, and Stump approached the group. Rake and Twig were arguing.

"There's no way you got more of them with your bow than I did with my slingshot," screamed Rake. "I've seen you throw a spear and you couldn't hit an ant hive with a tree trunk!"

"Say that again, Rake Raven, and I'll pin you to the back of a rat faster than you can chew cheese," Twig pulled back his bow, but Nut grabbed his arm.

"That's enough!" Nut said firmly. "The rats won't want him either."

Everyone laughed but Rake.

"Me lovelies wants whatever I tells them they wants," said Big Cheese, who came limping up to the group with the help of Shady, and then turned his attention to Leaf. "So, we's still has a deal there, my young leaf leader?"

"Leaf leader?" Shady grunted and dropped the rat where he stood. "He's no leader. He couldn't lead a moth to the light of a forest fire! In fact, he…" His words were cut short as Thicket Figthorn put his hand around his son's mouth.

"That's enough out of you," he said. "If it wasn't for Leaf, we would have been fighting the rats, too!"

"And you wouldn't have been rescued from the ants and wolf-spiders that caught you," said Garland.

"And we wouldn't be here in the first place," said Twig.

"To find a new land," said Principal Oakreach.

"And we wouldn't have known to come to your aid, if Leaf hadn't saved my boys," said the robin, who then turned to Rose. "I'm glad you leaf folk *get along* so well. I'd hate to see what it would be like if you ever fought amongst yourselves."

They all had a good chuckle except for Shady and Rake.

"We had better be off to help the others who came with us," added the robin. "And then it's back home for us. What will you do now?"

"I fer one will be a climbin' in me hole a spell," said Big Cheese. "I aren't feel'n up to no ship voyage jest yet—gots to let these ant bites heal. Maybe another day, but fer now I'll be lettin' whomever wants to go, go."

Rose took the robin by the wing and hugged her and then kissed her on the cheek. "Thank you," said Rose. "We'll be sailing on this ship to a new land. We have to find a place where there are plenty of trees."

"The Coastals found it once, and are going back there again," Eric said. Leaf turned to his father.

"Dad, what did you mean before when you said the Coastals found a new land but don't know what to do with it?"

"Well," Eric said, "They know what they *want* to do with it, but there are already others living there who don't want them chopping down *their* trees. They had a fight, it seems, and now the Coastals are going back to make peace and try again."

"Well, I hope they make peace, but don't get the trees," said the robin with a grin.

"Me too," added Rose.

"When you find this new land, will you please come back and let us know where it is?" asked the robin.

"I will, I promise. I'm Rose, by the way. What is your name?"

"I'm Grace."

Thank you, Grace, and your boys, and please tell the rest that we are all eternally grateful."

"I will," said Grace and off she flew with her boys by her side.

Rose then bent down to where Big Cheese sat in a heap where he lay since Shady dumped him. She licked her hand and wiped away the blood from his snout and kissed him.

"Thank you," she said, "for trusting my son and for fighting with us."

Big Cheese blushed redder than the blood. "You's is most welcome, my lady," he said. "Most welcome, indeed. And don't you's worry none about this ant mess on the ship. Me lads will clear it up so's no one knows we was even here." And with that, Big Cheese turned back to head down to the dock. He didn't seem to have much of limp anymore at all. In fact, he skipped happily like a flea on his way to a bear den for the winter.

"Come, Oakley," Rose said quickly, grabbing the principal by the hand. "Let's go tend to your leg below deck." She turned to Eric. "Honey, would you and Thicket please gather everyone together so we can set sail with the Coastals?"

"Yes, me lady," Eric said in Big Cheese-fashion, while sweeping his arm to the ground with flair.

"That's 'Me Darling Lady', to you, mister," she said and laughed. She turned to Leaf. "Come along, Son. There's a lot to do before we leave."

As the adults walked away, Leaf put an arm on Nut's shoulder, shook Twig's hand, and then turned to Garland who was starting to walk toward the stairs to go down below. Leaf wanted to give her a hug, but Shady stepped between them.

"Don't think this cruise is going to be a sight-seeing vacation, 'leaf-leader' Leaf," Shady said. "I'm gonna show everybody what a mistake it is to even think you could be a *leader.*"

Leaf simply turned to Twig as they walked. "Did you hear something, Twig?"

Twig wagged his head from side to side and said, "No, but I smell something."

Nut checked his feet to see if something was stuck to them, straightened his half-an-acorn helmet, and followed behind the rest as they headed below deck.

EPILOGUE

Later that evening, Leaf peered out from the rafters of the ship and watched as the Coastals stood along the docks to call farewell and to wave at their loved ones who were sailing away. He could tell that many were crying.

The vessel turned slightly to the north and, keeping to the coastline, was soon opposite the forest and what remained of its great trees. The last glint of green along the highest branches was all that was left of the daylight, and slowly fading, sadly resonated in the young boy's leafy veins.

"Good-bye," he muttered and raised his hand.

In an instant, Stretch hopped off of Leaf's shoulder, ran up to the top of his fingers and back down his arm. It tickled, but Leaf wasn't laughing.

"Not now, boy," he said and patted the little fellow on his head.

The next morning, Principal Oakreach found Leaf sitting and staring out of the same hole in the rafters. He sat down next to Leaf and handed him a blank piece of paper and a thin stick of charcoal.

"Here you go," he said, as he handed them to Leaf. "You'll need these to map out your next adventure."

Leaf looked at the blank paper and sighed. It seemed he was going to have to learn how to draw after all.

To be continued…

ABOUT THE AUTHOR

William Sells is a former newspaper journalist turned freelance marketing writer, and associate producer for Maryland Public Television. A published poet, songwriter, and short-story writer, he lives with his wife Yovi and their three daughters amidst the sprawling green parklands of Columbia, Maryland between Washington DC and Baltimore.

www.wgsells.com

ABOUT THE ILLUSTRATOR

Michael S. Bracco is the graphic novel author and illustrator of *The Creators*, the award-winning Novo series, and *Adam Wreck and the Kalosian Pirates Space Pirates*. Along with his comic work, Michael owns and operates "Spaghetti Kiss", a craft company that features his original science fiction and fantasy illustrations. Michael is also a part of the performance art group known as, "Super Art Fight" and spends his days teaching art to middle school students. He lives in Baltimore with his wife, Shawna, their daughter, Amelia, and their cats, Mexico and Stranger.

www.spaghettikiss.com